TALE OF THE WINTER LANDS

# TALE

## *of the*

# WINTER LANDS

J. D. Bass

*Tale of the Winter Lands.* Copyright © 2017 JD Bass.

ISBN: 978-1-7341664-0-8 (hardcover)
ISBN: 978-1-7341664-1-5 (paperback)
ISBN: 978-1-7341664-2-2 (e-book)

Library of Congress Control Number: 2019919916

Printed in U.S.A.
First edition, December 2019.

www.jd-bass.com

While with my head amongst the clouds of magic most of the time,
You were all here to support the silliness of my ever-stubborn
Mind. And I'm immensely grateful.
To Love, Family, and Friends

*The Dedication of this tale goes to every child, small or big.*

*To all the Little Angels lost too early, but never forgotten.*

*To all of those who Believe in the Beauty of our Dreams!*

*May you never lose that marvelous innocence—pure and childish.*

*Hold on to the happiness of your Heart.*

With love,
Mizan.
♡

# Contents

When you succeed in looking beyond the world of all-knowing technology and globalization, past any limit, far from relentless progress, you will discover a beautiful secret world of joy—a world filled with magic and splendid secrets of life itself. You will find the happiness interwound with unbelievable fairytales of which you have never even fantasized in your wildest dreams.

The story goes, well, something like this!

Merry Christmas!

Dear Diary,

Though three months early, my letter to Santa Claus is already written and addressed to whichever snowy address he inhabits—somewhere that my imagination is taking me, from Finland to the North Pole and to the Antarctic itself.

It doesn't have to be a specific place so long as there's handfuls of snow, tons of pine trees, and countless hidden places surrounded by ice, bathed in the winter sun.

Am I peculiar for still keeping up this tradition, even as a twenty-six-year-old girl—trying desperately to hang onto my innocent belief in something beyond what our eyes can see, by putting a little faith in the written words on a plain piece of paper?

While people are growing up, they tend to forget how to believe in something they can't see or touch. Why do people have this ever-present need to blame everything on America, accusing us of wanting to push our traditions on the rest of the world? Little do they know that the Christmas tradition started with a Greek bishop, a charitable man who helped children in need, who lived in Turkey and died on December 6: that is when much of Europe celebrates St. Nicholas Day. Later on, the same continent gave him magical powers like flight, and he appeared as a white-bearded man. America just gave Santa the cute, maybe too-chubby look and the red-and-white costume.

And reindeer.

I wonder who added sleighs to the whole look?

Anyhow, why am I writing this? It's like the student lecturing the teacher. Yes, I do that sometimes: I lose myself in words until my head starts to spin.

The most important thing is that I am, to this day, happy to share a one-of-a-kind, beautiful friendship with the tradition which has been imprinted on me ever since my first thoughts and feelings formed. Ah! Mom's knocking on the door! No more philosophy! Have to go! I'll write more later!

Kiss, Victoria

# Things Can Change . . .
# in a Flash

My mom didn't wait for me to open the door, she just came inside, ready with her questions.

"Victoria, are you still writing? Didn't you say you're going out with your friends?"

"Yeah, but I still have twenty minutes or so." I wasn't very fond of my mom's control-freak moments, but then again, she was almost always right. Just like now, when I had completely forgotten about the appointment but couldn't admit it to her. I'd never hear the end of it if I did.

"Who is going with you? Oh, never mind! But I sure hope you're going to change your clothes because this messy *holiday elf* look of yours is not for the public's eyes."

Even though I knew exactly how quickly my stupid remarks could make her angry, I simply had to ask, "Why not?" I couldn't hold my tongue.

"Well, you are wearing a holiday sweater with lights and the elf slippers three months before Christmas! We can manage your house style, but I don't think people outside are ready for it. And, Victoria? Please lower the music down, it's too early into the season to receive the complains about Christmas music." She just rolled her eyes at me and stepped out of the room, mumbling silently to herself.

I turned down the volume right away.

Of course, it hadn't even crossed my mind to go out without changing. But I loved to provoke my mom every once in a while. It's what kept her nerves in great shape.

Well, this is me . . .

I am Victoria. For friends and family, it's Vicky. I'll get straight to the point: I come from a wealthy family. We are fortunate enough to have everything we need but it wasn't like that when I was a kid.

The main difference between us and the majority of families in the Manhattan area is fairly clear—I don't want to offend anyone, but my parents went through a war when my sister and I were very young. Afterward, they created a life for us from scratch, while being carried on the wings of goodwill that people offered when we needed it the most. Mom, being a full-time writer, had time to take care of my sister and me, while our dad always worked hard enough to create something of his own. He still worked at his financial advising company, which is slightly bigger than before. Even though my mom isn't happy about him piling on working hours, the workaholic in him is stronger than anything; my dad doesn't seem to know how to stop.

Our parents taught my sister and me proper behavior, without privilege, from day one.

Well, there was one privilege . . . but only thanks to a good-hearted man, my dad's friend, who settled us in his hotel after we came to America to escape the war which was raging back home. He helped us without hesitating in the past when he offered the discounted rate for the apartment until my parents got back on their feet.

2

A good heart never ceases to amaze me.

We live in an apartment on the eleventh floor of One Plaza condominium. My favorite part of living here, without a doubt, is Central Park—a park where the four seasons leave their mark throughout the year. Anyone who lives in a huge metropolis surrounded by skyscrapers and hectic traffic and life will entirely understand what am I talking about: we yearn for a little freshness.

Let me tell you one more thing: nothing can beat Central Park winters, when fluffy snowflakes put all the trees and flowers into a two-month deep sleep, tucking the entire city into a beautiful white fairy tale.

Of course, not everyone likes winter, but I take a slightly brighter point of view and never complain about the wet snow.

"Victoria!" my mom shouted from the kitchen. The smell of freshly baked croissants filled the air. "Your friends are already downstairs! Are you ready?"

The way she always shouts instead of coming to tell me what's on her mind is something I'll never understand. It seems my mother likes to show off her lung capacity.

"Not quite yet! Tell them I'll be there in five!"

Usually, I beat a Swiss watch when it comes to punctuality, but this is the season when the people who know me are used to my daydreaming and forgetting things because in my free time I listen to music, watch Christmas movies, cook, or write in my diary. I still had to get dressed. Everything was already on my bed. I had prepared it the evening before. Together with my friends, Tom, Nicholas, Lisa, and Annabeth, I was going to the gala opening of the ice-skating season, and the best part was that we got to wear masks.

My transformation for this special occasion was Zorro, the female version of it. This look combined perfectly with the red shoes Aunt Maggie had bought me for my twenty-sixth birthday—because, of course, there was an 80 percent chance we were going to the club afterward. Obviously, I had every black detail, from the hat and cape, to the whip and silky laced mask that covered my eyes making me feel more comfortable about being dressed like this and walking with other lovely weirdos in the middle of New York City.

The only thing I didn't have in my possession was a fake sword, but Nicholas was taking care of it for me.

"Mom, I'm going now! Please tell Dad if I call him once it's a sign to pick me up at nine sharp, if he isn't too tired, but if I do it twice, we're going to the club, and I'll get an Uber. Kiss!" I ran like the Flash through the apartment.

I knew it wasn't kind of me not to take my sister ice-skating with us, but my friends wanted to go to the club afterward, and she's too young to enter one.

After the short elevator ride down, I zipped out the front door of the hotel. "Hey, Walter! How are your wife and kid?" As usual, I just flew past the doorman without waiting for the reply. But he understood; it was our daily routine.

I heard his pleasantly rusty sixty-five-year-old voice: "Everything's fine! Victoria, be careful on that ice, strange things are happening today!"

In front one of many New York's yellow cabs, Superman, Little Red Riding Hood, a police officer, and Tom were eagerly waiting for me. Actually, Tom was the only one who surprised me with his outfit, because he said he would never put on a disguise. Yet he had a huge stomach, an elegant black suit with the typical white pinstripes, his hair soaked in gel (which brought out a resemblance to his father), and a red rose in his pocket, along with white cotton inside his mouth, revealing his identity for the day: Don Corleone. Seeing my skeptical look, he put his hands up.

"I can explain! So, my mom always wants me to dress up like my dad, and all of dad's punchlines are about *The Godfather*, so for the first time in my life, I decided to make them happy and combine both. Voila, but just for one evening! I'm sure I don't have to tell you they had tears in their eyes and did a photoshoot before I left the house. Unfortunately for me—now they have proof. The only thing I couldn't go along with is the mustache." Tom shrugged his shoulders indifferently. Due to the cotton in his mouth, he was definitely talking like Don Corleone. "I've always hated mustaches!"

I didn't have to add anything.

"Girls, you look amazing!" I said to my female friends.

"Thanks!" Annabeth was probably the kindest and most honest human being on this planet—I couldn't tell if she was blushing or if it was part of the Little Red Riding Hood costume.

On the other side, Lisa made a great cop, looking gorgeous and in style. She was a well-known fashion addict. "I know, I know," she said, "my costume is not as original as theirs, but I feel more comfortable wearing a uniform. You know me!" To other people, Lisa sometimes seemed shallow because of her high-pitched voice and the way she planned each detail of her outfits, but she was also an intelligent student of architecture.

"Ah, Nicholas! Seriously?" I said to Nicholas.

He looked confused. "What's wrong?"

"Couldn't you have been Batman, Dr. Strange, Wolverine, Green Arrow? You had to be Superman like probably a thousand other people today?"

"I don't care. At least this way I don't need to wear a mask, so if you need me, you'll be able to recognize me from far away. And I like Superman's powers. Maybe his laser eyes could help me melt the ice tonight so we can spend some quality time somewhere warm." Sarcasm was Nicholas's trademark.

"Okay, okay! I give up!" I said.

On our way to Rockefeller Center, we talked about every topic possible: we didn't meet up often, as we were all at different colleges, grad schools or jobs.

"How come they opened the ice-skating season on Columbus Day?" asked Lisa. "It's been bugging me since the beginning of September."

"I wouldn't know. I did ask my dad about it, but as usual, he's not into finding stuff out." My father always said that family comes first, then business, and afterward, everything else. And he wasn't particularly interested in the third thing.

I kept my answers short out of respect for my friends. At this time of year, I had a tendency to finish absolutely every conversation with a Christmas-related topic, so I tried hard not to be the old me. I had promised myself I would talk less and listen more.

When we arrived at our destination, the magnificence of Rockefeller Center overcame me once again with its charm and left me speechless, unsure where to look first.

The entire skating rink was illuminated with small, bright LED lights in the form of snowflakes, and the rink's edges were decorated with large snowflakes made of fake soft feathers, from the smallest to the largest, which were over nine feet tall, connecting at the very end to create a beautiful arch with a silver 'Welcome' sign.

We watched a fantastic show on the ice, with professional ice skaters dressed as fairytale, cartoon, superhero, and movie characters, all accompanied by light notes from movie soundtracks. Their costumes were perfect, and they completely pulled us into the storytelling with their dancing. It was hard to tell the difference between imagination and reality, and their graceful movements, done with so much ease, kept us all entranced.

Oh, the Christmas tree? THE Christmas tree? It was even bigger and prettier than last year, with bordeaux and white decorative balls, feathery angels, stars, snowflakes, crystal icicles, and handmade ornaments from the local artists, in every imaginable shape.

"I'm amazed!" Annabeth squeaked out of happiness. I sat there with a silly grin on my face.

The event's organization was impeccable. They had tried to make it better than in previous years, and even the mayor's vastly shorter speech was a big surprise to everyone. Needless to say, it was the first year the crowd had ever given him a long, warm round of applause.

"The ice skating rink is now open for all! You may step on the ice!" a calm voice cut through the crisp air.

I didn't skate for long, but it gave me a sense of euphoria.

Suddenly, Tom abruptly took my hand.

"Vicky, did you see they have catering on ice? Can I bring you something to eat?" He couldn't help but talk to me like I was a little child.

"Oh, yes, please! Bring me two mini tuna sandwiches. I saw they have it on the menu. I skipped dinner tonight. I couldn't stop writing diary!" My stomach was growling at the mention of food.

"And bring me some donuts, please!" Lisa yelled, but Tom had already turned his back on her.

People smiling from ear to ear, their red cheeks pinched by the cold, danced with the slow, romantic music. When they stepped on that ice, they were truly themselves: relaxed and grateful they had the time to share happiness with other people.

I was moving slowly, just listening to the music and not thinking about anything else, when my thoughts were interrupted by the firm hand of the Flash.

"Dance with me, Victoria!" he said softly, taking me into the middle of the crowd.

*How did he know my name? How did he recognize me, when I didn't know him?*

Our parents teach us not to talk to strangers, no matter what age we are . . . especially in a city as big as New York. And it's even worse to dance with a stranger!

But this felt like an exception. There was something in his voice that told me I knew him somehow . . .

"I'm sorry I can't remember, but who am I having the honor to dance with?" I was confused, hearing my shaky voice and feeling the familiar goosebumps overtaking my body—not from fear, but from a weird connection between us, something private in his touch.

"Shhh, just let the magic of the moment speak for us!." His voice was in my memories somewhere, so soft, yet profound at the same time.

My instincts were screaming that I knew this mysterious Flash, and I wasn't entirely able to enjoy the moment while I was trying to figure out whose face was hiding beneath the Flash mask. In spite of the people around us, we dance-skated with such ease. His movements made my senses going off the charts with emotion and attraction.

Over his shoulders, I could see my friends giving me surprised looks. Tom waved his hands all over the place trying to gesticulate his questions.

I needed to break the tense silence as Flash and I danced to "Last Christmas." "Where do we know each other from?"

He smiled mysteriously. "Deep down, you know where . . . You're going to remember. Some things you can't forget, Vicky . . . at least not twice."

I still didn't understand. "Twice?"

My mysterious superhero hopelessly shook his shoulders, and with a little sadness in his voice, said, "You already forgot about me once. I sure hope it won't happen again." He twirled me and then disappeared into the crowd.

I have to admit; prior to this, I had been hoping for more mystery in my life, but this was completely unexpected.

Too nervous and confused to start searching for him, I went back to my friends, who fired question after question at me.

"Who was that dashing Flash?" Lisa was always the loudest person in the room. I could hear her voice from miles away.

"To be honest, I still don't know . . ." I was only half-aware of her interrogation, as my mind was rewinding the previous moments, trying to figure out anything that could help. Nothing.

"Has your mother never taught you talking to strangers is a bad thing, especially during nighttime in New York?" Tom couldn't hide his jealousy anymore. "In this crowd, he could've kidnapped you in a heartbeat!"

I usually didn't pay any attention to his behavior, but this time the sarcasm just came out of my mouth. We were twenty-six, and he was still treating me like a silly girl in front of our friends. "It would be impossible under your hawk-eye surveillance." The moment I said it, I wanted to take it back. It was the first time I had acknowledged his feelings. But in the embarrassment of the moment, the Tom-wants-to-be-my-boyfriend situation wasn't my priority. Sometimes I seemed heedless of his feelings, but that was only because he was my best friend and I wanted it to stay that way.

He knew better than anyone I wasn't completely over Brian. Tom was there for me, through tears and heartbreak, but just as the best friend a girl could ask for.

His face was completely red, not so much because of what I'd said, but because he was finally realizing I had friend-zoned him in an ugly way.

"I'm going to get a drink. See you later!" He left as fast as he could.

But my mind wasn't on him. It was still floating toward the secret Flash that knew me so well.

Nicholas was still talking: "Vicky? Earth calling Victoria!"

"I was just thinking how you're all right." It was a huge lie. "It's my mistake, and that won't happen again." False sincerity isn't usually my thing.

Anyhow, my friends were right. I knew that, obviously: my parents wouldn't have reacted any differently. They were trying to get me to see common sense.

Afterward, I avoided thinking about the Flash and concentrated more on my friends— except for Tom, who tried to evade my apologetic looks for the rest of the night. I decided to call it a day, so my dad picked me up. I just couldn't bear going to the club and enduring Tom's coldness. Because when he ignored someone, he took it to the limit.

A Black VW Tuareg stopped at the taxi station, and a familiar face with glasses was smiling at me.

"And how was it?"

"Great! It was better than I expected. Thank you for the tickets, Dad." I gave him an honest kiss on the cheek but wasn't planning on telling him what happened. Thanks to the dance with Flash, I was still in seventh heaven.

"No problem. I'll need the favor back, though."

"Ha! I knew there was a catch."

"You know me well." He smirked, but I could sense his concern. "Your uncle called yesterday to tell us Marc is finally marrying Maria, and he wanted to know right away if someone is available to come to the wedding."

"Wait, wait! Back it up, Dad! Marc is getting married? My favorite cousin is getting married, and I'm learning about it like this?" I couldn't hide my disappointment and anger. Maybe I had been wrong, and distance did play a significant role in human relationships after all, even if it involved family blood.

"Easy, Vicky. Why do you take everything to heart? They can't only be thinking of you; you two are thousands of miles apart. And your uncle did say they've tried to reach your sister and you a couple of times but they just couldn't. That's why he finally called me, his brother."

Apparently, Marc had finally got the courage up to take the important big leap with Maria three weeks ago, and the wedding had already been planned for the next month. Maria had just finished up the classes she had missed after a long period of soul-searching, they were living in their own apartment, and they had saved enough money to cover everything by themselves.

"Unfortunately, your mom and I have obligations with our jobs that can't be postponed, since we're obligated by contracts and deadlines, and your sister has a lot of college exams. We all know how your mom can sometimes be over-controlling with you both when it comes to college obligations. She wants to give you and Joanna all the attention she never had. That's why we thought we could send you to represent the family. Do you like the idea?" He was looking at me more than the road, so he slowed down. He knew I wasn't very keen on traveling by myself.

I was scared of traveling alone, and I never did—the day I would have to face it alone had come sooner than expected. But, in spite of my initial apprehension, I thought it was a brilliant idea. My mind immediately wandered to the relaxing break grad school, the fun that weddings usually provide, and the fact that I was about to visit Italy after a long absence.

"Okay, don't stress about it anymore. I'll gladly go."

I noticed a flicker of disappointment in my dad's eyes when he realized he couldn't do the rest of his Victoria-please-go speech. But then he just looked relieved.

By the time I had reached the house trailing my dad, my mom jumped up cheerfully, pleased with my decision, ready with a thousand questions about my wellbeing and my plans for the trip. She even suggested I should visit my home country while in Italy.

When I was just six years old, we came to New York from Croatia. There was a war at the time, so my mom and dad gathered all the necessary courage to go overseas with two little girls and start a new life, since we had lost every possession. Our love for our small country stayed strong, and every summer and sometimes even winter, we would go there to enjoy the beautiful Croatian coastline as well as the continental side, especially the capital city Zagreb during the Advent time.

Joanna, my younger sister, was bursting with jealousy. This was a family event she wanted to participate in, and I could understand her frustration.

After the typical angry outbursts toward me and our parents, she calmed down fairly quickly, not completely convinced they were going to send me there without her.

This time I didn't wait for the questions of how, when, and where. I ran to my room to call my friends and tell them the good news that couldn't wait for tomorrow. A lot of high-pitched screaming was involved.

Nervously, I started to dig through my closet, searching for what to wear, including warm clothes, since winter there was much snowier than in New York. The only thing I didn't already have was a dress for the occasion.

"Joanna! Oh, Joanna!" I imitated the voice of our mom. "Come to my room, please."

"Stop yelling and tell me what you need!" She couldn't hide her anger, so she waited five minutes to come to my room in personal protest.

"Will you go shopping with me?" I knew her weak spot. "Help me find a pretty dress for the reception, and I'll buy you something in return."

The moment Joanna heard the word *shopping*, a sneaky smile came back, and the sparkles in her eyes could brighten the entire room.

※

While I was waiting for the trip, I tried to do as much as I could to make the hours pass quicker than usual. If nothing else, this pushed the masked Flash out of my mind . . . But I didn't completely forget. I couldn't. *Not twice*, in his words.

Every minute, second, and hour was used wisely while my impatience for the trip grew stronger.

Italy, here I come!

And here is where the impossible became real.

# *Lost in Adventure*

When departure day finally came, nothing went as smoothly and efficiently as I had imagined.

How could I have forgotten to set my alarm clock?

All that planning, every little detail calculated, and then this? Well, that was so typically me.

And the worst thing was that my parents were wide awake the entire time, convinced they'd booked a later flight for me, so they let me sleep longer.

Nevertheless, forgetting to set the alarm clock was the dumbest thing I ever did.

The dumbest thing at that moment, at least.

At the airport, my stiff legs were in a race of their own, while my parents and sister were a long way behind me. Then I lowered my head for a second and the next thing I know—I bumped into the person in front of me.

"Are you okay?" I heard the concerned tone of a familiar voice.

"Yes, yes. It was my fault. I wasn't watching." For some reason, I felt ashamed, and I continued avoiding eye contact with the speaker. "I can't be late for my flight." I kept repeating this, never once looking at the person who so kindly helped me collect my items off the floor, including my plane ticket, which had fallen from my bag.

"Vicky, concentrate!" A stranger called out my name.

When I finally looked up, the familiar voice matched the face I had unconsciously been expecting to see: thick brown hair; beautiful eyes with their color balancing between green, yellow, and brown; firm long hands; and that lovely wide smile. I knew those details from long ago.

"Brian." I felt a sudden wave of heat intertwined with happiness, coloring my cheeks red.

No matter how much time passed, he always had the same effect on me. Maybe because I thought he had forgotten about me; it made the feeling of embarrassment considerably worse.

A slow-motion movie rushed through my head, with every memory we shared together from the moment my cousin had introduced us. One handshake meant everything, although we were very young at that time. There were some innocent kisses involved too, but . . .

How does something end even before it begins?

In a word, silliness. Then, he couldn't realize how much he meant to me . . . And we can say a little thing named *pride* was involved too. I don't regret a single second I had with him; they were precious unforgettable moments.

"Hey, Vicky." He snapped his fingers before my eyes. "Where did you go?"

"Brian, I am so sorry. It is great to see you, it really is, but I don't want to be late for my flight . . ." Those words weren't the ones I wanted to say, but I couldn't help the way I obsessed with small details—not even for Brian—and the compulsive part of me was thinking only about the flight.

"Okay, I won't keep you. Where are you going?" He lowered his gaze to the airplane ticket in his hands. "Oh, it's beautiful there; went there skiing last year. I'm off to Chicago, business trip. I don't know if you heard, but I'm a financial adviser . . . 5 years now, working for various companies. Lately I'm more on the road than home. It'll be two extremely long and probably boring weeks. When are you coming back?" With his every word I kept watching the seconds and minutes going by. There was no more time to chat.

"In two weeks or so . . . I'm going to my cousin's wedding. Brian, as soon as I come back, we could grab a cup of coffee, but right now . . ." The words just flew out of my mouth. I didn't stop for a second to ask why he wouldn't be at the wedding too. After all, my cousin and him had once been best friends. In fact, without their friendship, our romance wouldn't have happened in the first place.

"You really have to go," he finished my sentence. I was already running toward the gate attendant when I head Brian yelling behind me. "Victoria, your ticket!" He was waiving my ticket, though I could have sworn I'd put it in my bag. Maybe I had been bewitched by his charm. Of course, I also had been trying to keep my parents from seeing him. Due to the powerful love we had once felt, my parents were terrified he might take me away from them, college, and New York entirely. I suppose many parents share that fear.

Brian ran over to me, gave me the ticket, and then to my big surprise, gently pressed a kiss upon my lips. It was a tender moment that took me down memory lane. My mother, who had caught up now, spotted it with her eagle eyes, and I could see the disapproval on her face.

"Stay safe, kiddo!" He used to call me that. With that kiss, he had put me upon the same fluffy clouds, and it took the gate attendant calling my name twice to bring me down to earth.

"Miss, I'm afraid you're at the wrong gate," she told me after carefully checking the information provided on the ticket. "You need to go down there." She pointed. "Gate J24. Hurry up, there's still two minutes until boarding."

Again I was on the run, but now with new excitement. Although I'd been on the verge of boarding the wrong airplane, I was still happy, partly because my mother hadn't had the chance to ask me anything about Brian.

And I was confident she had the wrong idea in her head from that little scene, anyway.

My emotions only calmed when I sat down and prepared myself for a ten-hour flight. A playlist with my favorite songs—yes, including a hundred Christmas songs—was ready to help me sleep better and relax on the ride across the Atlantic.

I didn't overthink about what to expect upon my arrival in Italy. My mind was wandering elsewhere.

❄

My eyes were so tired that in the next half hour I found myself in a deep sleep, so heavy that an old gentleman had to wake me up once we landed. But after repeating to me three times in his language that we had landed, he tried to do it with a charming accent in broken English.

"Girl, came here. We go out," he told me. He used more gesticulations than words, but I got the message. I have found that older people have more difficulty speaking a foreign language, but you have to appreciate their good intention.

"Thank you so much."

Do I have to mention again that this was my first time ever traveling alone to Europe—to another continent? And how important is it to check your ticket all the time? I didn't. Well, now I do.

As I disembarked from the airplane in the middle of the night, there was no shuttle. It seemed like a rather small airport, surrounded by tons of snow whose almost diamond-white color gave additional shiny light to the bewildering landscape. Nothing here was familiar. Before my flight, I had checked the weather forecast, which had clearly said there weren't going to be cold temperatures in the Alps. They also hadn't mentioned any snowfall on the Italian weather site.

I was distracted by a game in which the snowflakes covered my coat rapidly, trying to make a snowman out of me.

*I guess the forecast made a mistake. Nothing strange, it happens all the time.*

*And why isn't there any shuttle available?*

With deep breaths of sharp air, I cleared my lungs of New York smog and filled them with vast quantities of oxygen. And here I thought a stale airport air would be the first thing to breathe in.

For me, it was nice to stand on the snowy ground this time of year, but it was rather unusual that I was surrounded by the snow.

The only clear path I was walking on was covered with little crystals of ice, so extra caution was needed. I heard people saying we had landed on a side runway due to of the heavy snow, and we had been lucky not to be delayed. Needless to say, the innocent white welcome from nature wasn't to everybody's taste.

*I wasn't expecting snow, but I'm glad it is here. Looks like Santa is already granting my wishes.*

I kept that thought to myself.

"Good evening."

At the entrance of the airport, a young man greeted us politely, with the same accent as the old gentleman.

I turned back, but I couldn't see anyone behind me. I guess my curiosity had made me dawdle and end up being the last to enter the airport.

"Welcome to Helsinki, Finland." The young man continued with his warm greeting, though I didn't exactly comprehend his words.

"Excuse me, welcome *where*?" My voice was shaking more than usual, but the word *Finland* hit me in my gut like a sudden sucker punch.

All of the color disappeared from my face, and the boy clearly noticed something had shocked me, rendering me speechless. He didn't even try to figure it out on his own. Instead, he urgently called the manager of the airport. It was a wild guess that I needed help, which later appeared to be correct since I didn't understand a word of the Finnish language.

I spent the next twenty minutes trying to explain to the manager how it was possible that I had ended up in Finland instead of Italy, but he was confused just the same. He politely kept saying there was no way that no one had asked or mentioned the name of the country to which I was actually traveling. And that did make sense. But I knew that thanks to the impromptu meeting with Brian, I had been fashionably late—which I hate—to boarding, and my entire family had checked the boarding pass. Somehow, I convinced the manager that it wasn't my fault and that he should check all the information back with New York. And let me tell you, when he finally did, he was more confused than ever.

JFK confirmed I had had a regular check-in and ticket for a flight to Italy, but for no apparent reason, five minutes before take-off, the boarding system had put me on a plane to Helsinki. They couldn't figure out, though, how the ticket for Finland ended up in my possession. On both sides, they unsuccessfully tried to get to the bottom of the issue, before coming to an agreement that neither of them knew or understood what had happened.

At least they found a way to resolve this uncomfortable situation without me needing to add any money to the next flight or even sending me back, which had been under consideration.

I was to take a flight from Helsinki to Aosta, and they would even cover my expenses of transit to a hotel and on to my cousin's house.

My anxious feeling finally disappeared once the solution was found. And I didn't want to ruin this overseas experience, so with deep and slow breaths, I calmed myself.

Another polite lady spoke to me: "We sincerely apologize, one more time, for all the inconvenience you suffered today. Have a safe flight."

"Miss Victoria, our officials will escort you to the right gate this time and make sure everything goes as planned. Thank you so much for your trust." The manager of the Helsinki airport shook my hand firmly, apparently happy I didn't seem angry.

And I wasn't. The airport staff had done their job quickly, and it wasn't even their mistake, but they helped with the JFK airport as much as they could. Above all, it was probably a computer glitch. The important thing was that everything had worked out fine, and I was finally ready to join my cousins in Italy.

I had enough time to make one call before my next flight, so I called home, since the airline had called my parents to check the exact information about the flight purchase. They were worried sick.

The cell phone didn't ring once from the other side, and my mom was already screaming in the earphone.

"Victoria, are you okay? Where are you now? Why didn't you call sooner? We have been out of our minds since the airport called us an hour ago! An hour ago! My heart went up to my throat when they said they were calling from the airport. Are you okay?" Mom continued with question after question, without even letting me answer. Dad and Joanna helped calm her down so I could speak.

"Mom, it's nothing. I'm okay, everything is fine. It was a small glitch in the computer and it is resolved now. Listen, my battery is dying, and I don't have time to charge it since I'm catching a new flight to Aosta. I'll call you as soon as I land, I promise."

Emergency or not, it was like she didn't hear a word I said about boarding a new flight and she drowned me out. "How is it possible that you ended up in Finland when your father and I personally checked the tickets we gave you?"

"Mom, please, you're asking me something the airport staff doesn't even know. Maybe when I unexpectedly collided with Brian . . . No, he was going to Chicago. Never mind, it was a mistake. I repeat it's okay now. I gotta go. Talk to you all later! Love you!" I hung up. If I hadn't, my mom's drama would have continued. But that's how all moms are: worrying about everyone.

I found myself running through the crowd again, this time across shorter distances because the airport was five times smaller than JFK.

The gate attendant looked at my ticket. "That way, Miss Victoria."

"But the manager said . . ."

"Yes, we know the whole story. The management just took you here to us so we can make sure you're on the right path this time." Both of them showed me the opposite gate after checking my newly printed ticket. I checked it too, and this time it was right.

"Flight Helsinki to Aosta, gate 34 . . ."

Momentarily, all I wanted after this exhausting experience was a warm and soft sofa with a cup of hot chocolate and a good book. I was one of those rare people who still loved a book in their hands more than on a piece of technology.

In my defense, I love technology too. Actually, my friends call me a tech freak, and I don't deny it . . . as long as there is still some kind of respect and nourishment for tradition and its infinite sources.

After I stepped out into that cold breeze, a kind older lady escorted me to the small hangar where a much smaller airplane was waiting just for me. No one had told me I was going to Aosta in a small private jet. Maybe that was supposed to be part of the surprise. But who cared? There was an open door waiting for me.

When I stepped inside, I couldn't believe what my tired eyes saw.

This was my first experience with a private plane, but I found it very odd that its interior design was utterly holiday-like, and it seemed like an exact replica of my dream.

The first thing that caught my eyes was the beautiful material the interior was coated with; everything was covered in bordeaux velvet, which my fingers were yearning to touch. That softness of one-way cut material, the tenderness of its fibers; I could recognize it blind-folded. My grandmother actually had a frazzled old sofa—which had been in her family's possession for generations—that she didn't like so she kept it in the attic. I often sneaked up there and lost my time just sitting there reading her old books that never saw daylight.

Absolutely everything in the plane was bordeaux red with spots of green, "royal" material. That was my grandfather's name for vel-vet. All the surfaces on the couch, seats, and even carpet were marked with golden hand-inwrought thread spelling out different kinds of positive words, such as *Felicity, Bliss, Love, Courage, Wisdom, Belief, Trust.*

It was handmade. Imperfections in the lines could be seen in spots, and a different style was used on each word. When I touched it, its harshness showed that it wasn't made of regular thread. It wasn't made out of silky material, but something more like small stone dots.

I had never seen anything similar to it.

*Maybe the airport didn't want bad publicity.*

*Everyone knows that bad news travels much faster than good.*

*It would almost seem like they had borrowed the jet from a wealthy person with a singular taste in interior design.*

None of my thoughts seemed good enough to be true; something strange was happening to me on this trip.

On the other hand, I was happy as a child, and a joyful, prin-cess-y feeling was bursting out of me. Once I settled on the plush sofa, which was a strange thing to find in the middle of an airplane, I searched my whole bag to find my favorite birthday gift: the best smartphone ever when it came to taking photos. My need to capture the tiniest details was overwhelming—not just to show them to others, but for myself, to make sure this was really happening.

One of the details that caught my eye was an unusual wooden table, right next to the couch. Its legs were in the shape of tree branches

which were intertwined with winter red holly all the way to the top, from where the sweetest odor hit my nose and stomach. There was a white porcelain cup of hot chocolate. The smell of fresh cocoa reminded me of my childhood: slow, longing moments throughout the autumn for the winter season. On the couch nearby, there was a book whose covers I could've recognized anywhere. And I wasn't wrong. The original edition of *Anne of Green Gables* was waiting for me, already opened on the same page where I had stopped reading at home a couple of days earlier.

Strange but true, everything I could ever have wished for just minutes earlier was waiting for me here, while I maniacally took photos.

My mind was lost in a sea of questions until the pilot entered to introduce himself. There was no steward or stewardess on the plane.

"Miss Victoria, we'll be takin' off soon. Just make sure to have the seatbelt on and relax. If you feel slight turbulence, nothin' to be worried 'bout. We have a snow blizzard in front that's waiting impatiently for us. But everything is under control."

Judging by his looks, the pilot was ready for retirement. His uniform was like he had just come from the 1940s, his hair was hidden under the hat full of medals — odd place to put them, and his grumpy voice was far from soothing.

"Isn't it safer to wait for the storm to pass? The airport usually cancels the flights in that case. I'm definitely not rushing anywhere, and I'll be more than happy to wait."

But it was like he barely heard me.

"No questions? Okay. I'll leave ya to your readin' then, and ya'll leave me doin' my job." The pilot seemed clearly offended by my questioning, so he shook his gloved hand in disbelief and locked himself in the cockpit.

His aggressive tone and perfectly spoken English, with a strange southern accent, altered my mental state more, and I was troubled by a weird sensation during the entire flight, one that not even hot chocolate could ease. Because of the strong wind, the plane had some trouble moving forward without shaking. On top of that, I had been prohibited from using technology, a warning which the pilot bluntly communicated through the speakers. He didn't even dignify me with his presence after that first meeting.

❄

After two hours of flying, we were still up in the air, even though we should have been be on Italian soil forty-five minutes earlier; that was undeniably what was written on the ticket I was squeezing too tightly in my hand.

The pilot was the only one who knew why that was so, and he clearly didn't feel like chatting.

For a while, I continued with monologues in my head and possible scenarios. But then, all of a sudden, the pilot burst in with the biggest smile on his face.

"Miss Victoria, I am more than 'appy to tell ya, we have landed safely. Your luggage has been sent to its destination already. I hope you won't feel too offended by me saluting ya here and not showing you the way out since you already know . . . And frankly, being a steward is not in the description of my job. I must rush to somewhere, and thanks to you I'll be almost two hours late, and let me tell ya, I'm never late. Good evening."

I was confused. How could've I miss the landing part? Maybe I've dozed off for few minutes without noticing it.

So, he virtually threw me out of the plane. He just went back into the cabin and, without turning back, locked himself in.

Very rude.

Outside there was a raging snowstorm. I was lucky enough to have a long, warm coat to help me fight the cold. I was still confused as I left the plane. I'd already forgotten what the pilot had said about the luggage.

The pilot yelled from the cockpit: "The luggage is already at its destination. G'nite." And he closed the main door abruptly.

*Why didn't I ask him about his weird behavior?*

So, it had happened again. Confused beyond reason and without being able to see my own finger in front of my face due to the low visibility from the storm, I stepped bravely forward, not knowing what to expect. Then the unthinkable unfolded before my eyes, once I had a clear view in front of me.

I usually considered I had a loud voice, but now it broke in my throat, and I swallowed the scream, speechless. There was absolutely nothing in front of me: no airport, people, or path leading anywhere. It was just me and the howling mountains. I was alone, standing in the middle of a small freeway, with barely any lights except ten small LEDs that marked the path for the plane, which was . . . *gone*. How could it be gone without me having noticed the small jet leaving, or even hearing the sound of it taking off?

The temperature outside was probably negative twenty degrees Celsius, as the first tear froze instantly on my cheek. My body, which really wasn't used to polar frosts, suddenly became weak.

# Wonders of the
# Winter Lands

I was alone, in a foreign country that probably wasn't Italy, not knowing the language, and I was in the middle of nowhere. No civilization. No transportation. No nothing.

Now I couldn't fight the fear anymore. It consumed me instantly. The snow quickly covering me wasn't helping.

"What's going on? Oh my God . . ." I couldn't control my thoughts anymore—this was the weirdest thing that had ever happened to someone. I kept telling myself it was okay to cry over my unknown destiny. But I was too afraid to make any sound.

The phone I held in my hands wasn't showing any signal—I put it away in a warm side pocket so it wouldn't break in the ice-cold weather. There was no way of calling for help. Tears were flowing down my cheeks unabated, becoming ice as they did, which tightened my skin to the point of uncomfortable pain.

"Don't worry, Victoria." I comforted myself with a soft voice so it couldn't echo. "Someone will come for you. They must come for you."

The loud whistling of the wind that was trying to break through the woods and millions of dense flakes, was far scarier than the high white mountains which motionlessly stared at me.

All the blood in my body seemed to freeze when, behind a tall pine, I noticed a large dark shadow slowly coming my way.

But my astonishment was compounded when I saw that same mysterious shadow moving from all four legs to two. My eyes met the shiny eyes of a massive brown bear, and my scream finally broke through the landscape, creating five small echoes in a repeating melody. Fear racked every fiber in my body, and I fainted on the snowy ground.

I didn't know how long I had been unconscious. When I woke up, unable to open my eyes frozen shut by tears, I felt warm hands on my head, trying to bring me back to my senses. Vaguely, I saw a shadow taking me into its enormous arms, wrapping me up with a warm coat, giving me a sense of security. It was like I was in front of the fireplace, and hot air from the flames was bathing my body. The person carrying me smelled of dry wood, and he had a deep rusty voice that soothed me.

"Take it easy, Victoria . . ." It seemed he was the second stranger who apparently knew my name. "You'll have to forgive us. We have slight problems in communication these days. There was no reason for this to happen, especially to *you*, probably the second-most important person to set foot in the Winter Lands." The words spilled from his mouth, without taking a breath. He continued to mutter with traces of anger in his voice, only to address me once again.

"But I did warn him, Vicky, at least ten times. I said clearly 'Tommy, in exactly fifteen minutes, you have to go with Grandpa A to pick her up.' And I did mention I couldn't go because, well . . . Oh, obvious reasons. But no. Still, after he gave his promise, what happened? You were waiting here, all alone, freezing to death, just because some stupid rabbit with hearing problems changed fifteen minutes to fifty. Like I would ever say such a thing. Those silly rabbits. They only listen when it's about something of extreme importance to them and their businesses. You don't even know how lucky we are that only one of them has the gift of your language. Imagine what would happen to the Winter Lands and the people in it if they could all speak. Oh, no! I don't want to even think about it." Clearly irritated, he continued to ramble on about the talking rabbit called Tommy. *Does this man breathe between sentences?*

Still unable to see, my ears were struggling to link what I'd heard with any kind of common sense or even to believe it was real. Was it possible that after all this trouble I'd ended up in the hands of a lunatic living in the middle of nowhere? At this point, why not? I had flown over the ocean, only to be dumped twice in wrong countries, with tickets that said my name that weren't purchased by me nor by my family.

Minutes later, I gained control over my lips by moving them slightly, but as usual my tongue worked faster than my brain.

"You're not some kind of maniac lurking in the woods?" Honestly, I didn't even know how I'd found the courage to ask such a stupid question.

My savior laughed so hard that the mountains sustained it with strong echoes. "Do you think I would say yes if so? Let me tell you, I wouldn't." And he continued with genuine laughter, which made me feel worse than before. "This world is taking an ugly turn when a stranger can't help you when you fall without being called a maniac or being told that he must have done it for a hidden purpose. It is like all of the goodness is slowly disappearing, and we don't move a muscle to change it. No, Victoria. I am a strange person, one of the weirdest you'll ever have the chance to meet, but I am certainly not bad. Crazy merging with brilliant, yes."

My mind was trying to catch up and process all the information.

"Did I arrive in Italy? Why aren't you speaking Italian?" I was trying to buy some time until I managed to open my eyes.

My savior noticed me struggling to open them, so he put his fluffy sleeves on my eyes, helping to warm them enough. It was clear he meant well.

"Thank you."

"Now, if you want me to speak Italian, I am a bit rusty, but I can manage. Actually, there are a lot of other languages I'm better with, like German, French, Finnish, Russian. You name it. It is in my job description."

*Did he work in a hotel or other tourist spot?* "You still didn't answer my question. Are we in Italy?" Giving up wasn't an option, so I added a few white lies. "Tomorrow is my cousin's wedding, and the entire family is waiting eagerly for me."

"Victoria," he started sharply and a bit disappointed in me. "Didn't your parents teach you lying is bad? Always tell the truth. To your generation it may seem like a cliché, but it is far from it. Truth, no matter what. Maybe it won't bring you popularity among people, but at least you'll be known as an honest woman with integrity. Use it more often." With just a few words, the stranger made me feel not only upset with him, but also that I had betrayed everything my parents had taught me. All because of a little white lie. How was that my fault? But then, I started to think differently and felt sorry for being shallow, something I wasn't usually willing to admit. And that frightened me.

"I don't know what . . ." I couldn't calm my nerves.

"Your cousin is getting married in two weeks. Trust me when I say, you'll be there on time, if not before. We are extra cautious when it comes to the details." I was alarmed by how much he knew about me. "To answer your question: we are and we aren't in Italy. It depends on how you look at it." Everything he said was a riddle.

Finally, my eyes popped open underneath his coat.

"How? How? I was supposed to be in Aosta. What's going on today?" It was really difficult for me to take his hand off my face because it was unusually heavy, but I definitely wasn't ready for another shock.

My voice twisted into a horrific scream.

Because I now saw my savior lacked human features, and that the warm coat sleeve was actually the big paw of a bear. My intense Hitchcock scream clearly startled him too, so he opened his arms, and I fell into a big pile of ice-cold snow. Even that didn't stop me from screaming. But the realization that the 'bear' hadn't eaten me and that he could speak caused my fear to diminish.

"Are you okay?" My savior repeated the same question at least twenty-five times until I realized he was talking to me.

"Animals don't talk. I must have fainted and now I'm having this crazy dream." I was talking out loud to myself, trying to pinch my cheeks and arms. But everything just hurt.

I didn't bow my head nor lower my gaze as I kept looking at the same scene before me: a standing and talking bear with his worried face that kept asking me if I was okay. And it wasn't a toy, or anything explainable. It was a bear that was talking to me. A talking bear.

"Am I on a hidden camera or something? Did my parents rent you to do this? You can't be a real bear. This isn't funny. Someone please slap me in the face so I can wake up." That probably wasn't one of my smartest ideas.

The bear looked at me surprised, with one eyebrow raised, and a questioning look.

"Hm, are you sure that is what you really want? Because they did tell me, 'Her every wish is your duty.'"

"Yes." The small affirmation escaped my mouth without thinking about the words that I had spoken.

"But, Victoria, my paw is truly heavy. Are you sure?" There was a small hint of pride in the bear's voice.

"Yes."

"Victoria . . ."

"Right now!" I jumped off the ground and stood angrily before him.

The moment I lifted myself from the ground was the same moment the weight of his gentle slap threw me back down. And I could tell that for him it was as though he had barely touched me.

It was my wake-up call.

"I can't believe this is actually happening to me."

"Well, of course, it is real. I already told you how that annoying rabbit and Mr. Avery forgot to pick you up. It was a miracle I was off duty this evening . . ."

"Ooh, no, you won't!" I was courageously pointing my finger toward the bear. "You won't suck me into your ridiculous stories. What am I, Alice in Wonderland?" My body was shaking with anger while the bear was looking at me like I was the crazy one.

"Of course you're not. That story is beyond inspiring. So beautifully written by Lewis Carroll. Inspired, extraordinary." His tone of voice, and accentuated words, made me believe there was something more he had to say about it. Yet he skipped it. "What's going on here is a reality that doesn't have its story written. Not yet."

No! I had had it with the half-explanations from this bear calmly standing on two feet and talking to me in some unknown place. A few moments ago I had been surrounded by people, technology—even an annoying pilot seemed like honey compared to this illusion—while now I was talking to a bear that laughed and spoke, who acted with pride, and even took offense.

"Okay. You're a bear. I'm a human being. You're the bear. I am a human being. I am a walking, talking human, and you're . . . the same? No. That can't be right."

The bear laughed honestly. "Why not, Victoria? I still breathe, eat, sleep, and roar instead of talking. But here, where you can perfectly understand, I can be myself . . ."

Although everything seemed like a dream, I decided to play along to learn more.

"And where exactly is 'here'?"

We were walking fast now, deep in the woods, between giant pines and steep cypress trees, on a carved-out path surrounded by three-foot walls of snow. The air was pure, filling my lungs with freshness while colors played hide-and-seek with snowflakes in the sky.

Then a unique thing happened: I could have sworn the snow was continuing to fall behind us, but it stopped in front. Only then did I clearly see that those colors in the sky were the Aurora Borealis, the magnificent northern lights I had been wishing to see since I was five. I could check that off my bucket list.

Carefully following the light trail that was moving so elegantly, in the rhythm of the Viennese Waltz, across the sky, I forgot to ask any more questions, as I was overwhelmed by nature and its beauty.

Dream or not, the scenery felt breathtaking and absolutely real.

"Before we continue with your interrogation, let me introduce myself. I am—" a slight uneasiness was revealed in his cough "—Rudolf."

Although he was trying to sound firm, it didn't stop my spontaneous giggle at the mention of his name.

"Be my guest. You may laugh as hard and long as you want, but let me assure you, reindeer aren't the only ones named Rudolph. I'm living proof. And above all, my name is Rudolf with an *F*."

Now I couldn't stop laughing no matter how I tried.

"Aha! Like there are no rabbits named Tommy." I managed to catch my breath again. "Let's get back to what you can prove. If we're not in Italy, where are we?"

Rudolf looked at me like I just had just fallen off the tree, and he was wondering why I still couldn't understand what he had been trying to explain for the last half hour.

"Ah, Victoria, how can I put it in simple words? Right now, you're everywhere! Including Italy."

And just when I thought it couldn't become any weirder . . .

"Excuse me?" The bear had me so confused that I almost hit the bent pine branch in front of me.

"I'm not a smooth talker as Mr. Avery or Sean was . . . is . . ." a shadow of nostalgia crossed his expression ". . . but I'll do my best. We are on every continent right now, Vicky. The Winter Lands is a marvelous place connecting all the winter places in one: mountains, lakes, waterfalls, hills, meadows, and forests of this world linked by nature's purest creation—snow. This place has no end, and all the sceneries here become united, regardless of the distance that separates them in your learned reality. Mountains pour into the hills, forests hide the most beautiful lakes with unique waterfalls, and there are barely visible lines between ice and snow meadows, day and night, shadows and sunshine rays. Life here is pure happiness, a sanctuary where we do good for the rest of the world and where, in only a few steps, you can go to another part of the continent to feel a different harmony or time of day. Here, Victoria, imagination and reality have no division. They are one and the same."

When he saw my confused look, Rudolf decided to explain it better, but he told me that first he wanted to take me to a place called Christmas Point of View.

"Christmas Point Of View? What is it? Where is it? Is it a Christmas tree, or a town?" I kept pilling questions out of excitement but Rudolf just smiled. He didn't want to ruin the surprise.

More than twenty minutes of walking got me pretty tired—going through the snow is the best cardio.

Finally, we reached a small open space with only one tree in it.

Another bucket-list item checked off.

"Victoria, let me introduce you to General Sherman. Dear General Sherman, this is Victoria."

Before me, one of the biggest, tallest, and widest sequoias in the world was standing at two hundred seventy-five feet tall.

"Remember, no boundaries here."

But I wasn't paying attention to Rudolf any more. Even though I was tired, my legs automatically ran toward the sequoia, as though it was an old lost friend.

Carefully, with my palms, I touched its bark, which contained in its roughness the past, present, and future. The sequoia, the royal tree, revealed in its perfectly crisp folds that this was reality. And it was as real as the air I was breathing. I was circling around the tree, wide in diameter, never taking my hand off it, trying not to miss a single detail.

While my dizzy mind was increasingly lost in admiration for the tree and the charms of life, Rudolf's patience was slowly draining. I realized he was still talking to me, but I was completely occupied with a small, almost invisible bulge on the tree's bark. It was in the shape of a star, near the gap at the bottom of the trunk. My fingers slowly explored the star's edges, then I pushed it with my palm in the middle, provoking a chain reaction inside the tree that made me step back in fright.

A rasping sound started, becoming louder, and I could clearly hear there was a mechanism of some kind inside the tree.

Rudolf was staring at me with awe once again. That made me uncomfortable; my cheeks blushed pink.

"What's going on?" I asked, panic-stricken, taking two more steps back just to be sure. Just then a narrow gap in the tree opened, revealing plain wooden doors wide enough to fit one person.

"Shall we?" Rudolf pointed happily to the doors with his big clumsy paw.

"Where?"

The bear looked toward the sky and took in a dramatic breath before saying, "Among the stars." He said it as though he had been planning to say this sentence for days.

We entered the wooden elevator, which was wholly handmade to the smallest detail. As we were in the middle of the forest without any electricity, I couldn't imagine how it could work, but then again, I was in the company of a talking bear named Rudolf.

From each side, the elevator was scratching the insides of the tree as we slowly started to ascend. Somewhere in the middle of the ascent, snowflakes began to enter the elevator in a fluffy slow-motion kind of way, and the front door somehow turned into transparent glass.

"Don't worry. The doors are still wooden on the outside." Rudolf supported me and held me up as my knees had lost their strength.

The snowflakes on my face, along with the sheer doors, which clearly revealed the scenery beneath us, made me feel like I was flying through the clouds.

We stopped abruptly with a thump.

"Victoria, I know about your fear of heights, and do forgive me for bringing you here, but this is the quickest way of explaining where you are. Just hold on to me, and everything will be okay. Trust me; soon enough, you will forget how high off the ground you are."

Rudolf wasn't great at calming people down, and mentioning my fear didn't help, but he was at least trying.

"Just out of curiosity . . . are we about fifteen, twenty feet off the ground?"

"Hmmm . . . It's more like the same height as the tree . . . Didn't you notice we are on the top already?"

When he pointed that out, I lost my balance. I looked up to see clear sky above us, and didn't have any chance to complain or escape when he pushed me out through the doors.

From the top of General Sherman, where we were bathed in mountain freshness, the view in front of us was simply astonishing!

On one side, far away from us, there was a landscape filled with emerald-green forests, frozen lakes protected by the reflection of the same polar brilliance, and giddily high mountains whose tops were lost somewhere between the clouds. On an entirely different side, a snowstorm ruled, dividing a giant lake with a white curtain from a forest that was lit in the winter sun.

The top of the tree had a wooden platform in the shape of a star, the same shape as the button below, and surrounded by a strange pointy fence. The moon battled the orange skies, in spots bringing the light upon us.

"Victoria, can you see that scary mountain range that goes through four layers of clouds, maybe more?" Rudolf asked. I couldn't see it because it was too dark. He had forgotten I didn't have the same sharp vision animals do, but then he gave me a pair of green binoculars.

"A bear with binoculars? Go figure." Rudolf decided to ignore my comment.

"We are on a star platform situated at the top of the sequoia in the middle of an unknown forest. Apparently on all continents at once, with a wooden elevator that works by magic. Did I leave anything out?" I whispered to myself.

After I looked through the binoculars, I realized some of the scenery was a long way from us. And the mountain chain Rudolf was talking about seemed never-ending; with its vastness blocking everything beyond it.

"My dear Victoria, you're now looking at Mt. Everest!"

Any words I could have replied with stuck in my throat. I had to hold onto the fence, so I wouldn't fall over and off the tree. Rudolf only just caught me at the last moment. But it still didn't stop him from talking.

"Down there, where you see the sunrise? That's the Russian valley, beautiful beyond any other. All those lakes intertwined with pine forests and polar lights? That's Finland, where you landed the first time; only it was too far away to pick you up quickly enough. You see, while you are in the Winter Lands, everything is connected and easier to reach, so a misunderstanding is still just that—a misunderstanding. Blame it on the rabbit. Anyhow, where was I? Ah, yes. Over there, where you can see the perfectly uneven mountain chain? Those are the lovely Alps."

I was mesmerized with the scenery and the fact I could see all the world's most beautiful places connected together. However, I didn't understand how did they travel when everything was covered with snow, and I didn't see any concrete roads or railroads.

"There is a special way of traveling, not including the sleigh rides. But you will learn about it later. Nobody has a transportation system like the Winter Lands."

Rudolf clearly felt proud of the Winter Lands, it almost sounded like it was the first time for him too.

"Ah, I could continue to list every winter wonder indefinitely . . . the Winter Lands is a huge community of everything pure on this earth." He laughed like a child.

I involuntarily closed my eyes. It was definitely too much information for the brain to process. *This has to be just a beautiful dream.*

When I've opened my eyes again, I started to do the same thing I had done as a kid: catch falling snow with my tongue. That made me realize I was thirsty, but Rudolf was prepared for anything. Without speaking my need, he climbed down one branch of the tree to get two small icicles, which he gently gave to me. I was surprised Rudolf knew what I needed in this moment.

"There is no traffic or dirt here. You can take those until we reach our destination, because the sources of fresh water are far from here, or frozen, which is a sad thing actually. I wanted badly to show you Thousand Creeks Meadow. But I was warned not to use the RushUp

Tubes right away."

"What are those?" I interrupted his talk, naturally I wanted to know more about the tubes but it seemed like he didn't have any intention of explaining it to me now.

"You would've loved it, but I guess it will have to be some other time. Our destination is more important. Rest is what you need now."

All I heard through the fog of confusion was the word *destination*.

"Can't you just magically make more water?" I asked. "I feel dehydrated . . ."

Rudolf stopped me there.

"Victoria, I am honestly sorry to disappoint you, but I am no Gandalf, if that is what you are thinking. Though it's kind of flattering, I am just a bear. C'mon now, there will be enough time for sightseeing. We have to move along."

Although the view from the canopy was stunning, I was happy to be safely on the ground.

It seemed like we were doomed to walk through the snow without stopping, but soon enough, we reached a narrow path that became wider with each step. Somebody had definitely been cleaning it because there was no fresh snow on the ground. We finally found ourselves at an open spot, where my attention was drawn to intense, almost fluorescent lights coming from a bright tunnel which pierced a big hill, and looked as though it was without end. Rudolf explained it was a shortcut to our destination.

The tunnel had signals, as you might expect, but they were far from normal. Unusually tall road signals—red-and-green columns, each with a tied silk bow—gave directions for pedestrians, reindeer, and sleigh rides.

I had been periodically rubbing my eyes from the moment I left the plane. Now, once again, I thought the lights were deceiving me, but no. It was all real.

The tunnel's interior had a superb speaker system that was

playing one of my favorite songs, "Baby It's Cold Outside," loudly. The lights were synchronized with the music, and the intensity of the music provoked a small snowslide, but Rudolf pulled me out of the way at the last moment.

Because of the icy glaze on the ground, I held on to the guardrail. It appeared slippery, but upon touching it the guardrail was actually sticky with a familiar powerful, sweet odor.

"It's not a simple guardrail. This one is made out of leftover candy canes. But do me a favor and don't try to lick it to see if I'm telling the truth."

"The thought didn't even cross my mind." I had learned that licking the icy guardrail with my warm tongue would be foolish, since my sister's friend had tried to lick the ice off a street lamp a long time ago. It had ended in tears and great pain after spending almost an hour trying to pull him free.

As we walked through the tunnel, my legs became like lead from the cold. I was exhausted and the tiredness started to kick in.

"Victoria, just a bit farther and we are there!"

Big flashy red signs confirmed he was right. We were about to end one adventure and enter a new one, but I wasn't sure I was ready for whatever was waiting under the bright sky ahead.

As we left the tunnel, I once again was struck by the Aurora Borealis playing her game above us, hypnotizing me with her beautiful light show in the sky filled with green, yellow, purple with black bands.

Rudolf gently nudged me and I diverted my gaze from the light show above. Down at the end of the path was a charming, brightly lit town spreading over the land. It seemed endless. I started to cry.

I was overwhelmed by the sight of this little town, as I was by everything that had happened to me since I left New York.

Prodded forward, perhaps by the smell of freshly baked apple pie and hot chocolate mixed with cinnamon, or the warmth that was caressing my entire body, my feet carried me down the hill as fast as

they could through the deep snow. That was until I stumbled over a small tree I hadn't noticed. As a consequence, I ended up falling and sliding on my back, all the way to the bottom.

I heard Rudolf's worried scream. He tried to catch up by running after me, but he tripped over the same tree and slid downhill, ending up with his head in the pile of snow next to me.

We were both out of breath, but we still managed to laugh. Nevertheless, the bear gave me a reproachful look. He didn't need to say anything.

"I know. I promise I'll try to be careful next time."

After standing and shaking off the snow, the town captured my attention. Impeccable geometrically distributed street lights with their romantic, warm yellow light illuminated the streets in all their splendor.

The bronze-colored street lamps were almost thirteen-feet-tall and didn't look like any other lamp I'd ever seen before. Each one had stories carved on it.

"Aaahh, I should have known those," Rudolf gestured toward the nearest lamp, "would mesmerize you. These lamps, Victoria, are one of a kind, carefully handmade from copper, so they could last . . . forever."

"Handmade? Are you sure?" The lamps looked too precise, too perfectly sharp in their details, which I couldn't imagine someone carving by hand.

"Of course, I am. Every story you see here represents some winter or Christmas story that has been told but never written down. No matter if it was told by a five-year-old child who still doesn't know what storytelling is and he's making it all up, step-by-step with pure childish enthusiasm, revealing the smallest imperfect details to his imaginary friend; or if it came from somebody's grandmother who was trying to put her grandchildren to sleep by telling them a short bedtime story."

"If that's so . . . then there are millions and millions of stories in every possible language!"

"We do have the exact count somewhere, only I don't know it. I remember that people of the Winter Lands were always worried about the space for the future stories . . . But today, stories like those filled with love and possibilities, about magical winter or Christmas adventures, are disappearing as the world changes."

"How come you don't have millions of lamps everywhere?"

"Ah, that's my girl. You have a sharp eye. It would be too crowded, and it would mess up the city's aesthetics. But we do have some houses, factories, and stores with stories on their walls, and sometimes on their roofs. In the Winter Lands, there is always a way!"

In spite of my preconceptions, my mind was finally starting to accept the reality of what was in front of me.

Softly, I slid my fingers over the writing on the lamp. They were indeed carved by hand: I could tell by the feel of it. Cute illustrations were accompanied with all kinds of different lettering styles telling the previously untold stories.

On the bottom of one copper lamp, there was a mysterious signet: WBnFamily

"This family must be so proud of their work! It takes a lot of patience to do such a thing, and I didn't realize people still cherished the old trade."

Rudolf laughed at me. "Original storytelling carving is something unique that only the Winter Lands has, but it didn't start with the human hand. Here you have to think more open-mindedly. The word *family* doesn't just belong to humans. Animals have their families too. This unusual and special tradition was started by a small intelligent family that goes by the name of Winter Bunny Family. Their entire name is Winter Bunny Jumptrade Family, but they decided to, and I quote, 'keep it simple'."

Rudolf succeeded in making me see that my thinking was too black and white, and it made me ponder when I had lost the rest of the colors.

*When did I start to be so narrow minded?*

What an eye-opener this place was.

"The letters seem so alive. As though they are moving. Can it be?" Each second I spent in the Winter Lands got me more confused, and now I was questioning everything I knew.

"Yes . . . Sometimes when a new story is in the making, other letters are slowly dancing along. I'll teach you later." Rudolf was watching me closely. "This is amazing! The very second new people come here, they get that blissful look about them. Oh, priceless."

Under our feet, grew a light green grass, exuding spring freshness and the smell of a mowed lawn.

"How come the grass isn't covered with snow like everything else here?"

But the answer appeared right in front of me. A bunch of chunky red chipmunks started to jump frantically over the lawn. On their striped backs, they had the tiniest vacuum cleaners in the shape of pinecones, which reminded me of car air fresheners, just cuter, while they hurried to vacuum the newly fallen snow.

"C' mon, chipmunks. Move it. Move it. Move it!" One of the chipmunks was especially energetic. Judging by the little gold star that was bigger than her hat, she was the leader.

"Victoria, don't get me wrong, animals here don't suddenly receive the gift of talk. In this place, we understand each other: we are united like the rest of the world should be, but we have some limits too."

He lost me; my concentration was entirely on the chipmunks. "She is soooo sweet." But as I knelt down near the chipmunk, I discovered in the most painful way that these weren't the friendly ones.

The chipmunk dug her long, sharp claws into my index finger that was going toward her chubby face. "Ouch! That hurts!" I said.

"Don't touch me! I'm not a toy. Let's go, chipmunks. MOVE IT! Faster. Time is measured in acorns. MOVE!"

They disappeared into their little pine-tree houses which were an exact replica of the Winter Lands' homes, down to the last detail.

"Rudolf, why do some animals talk and others don't? Isn't that wrong?"

"Victoria, you have an excellent eye . . . and ears. If people could understand every animal on this planet, it would become chaos. Trust me, as animals we have enough problems with fast squirrel talk or bunnies' nonsense and birds' mockeries . . . And we are the ones who are used to it. Our life is far more relaxing, interactive, and devoid of rules, making us more able to adapt to your customs rather than the other way around. Especially in the Winter Lands—"

Someone suddenly grabbed my hand firmly, raising it high up above my ear and twirled me three times, taking my breath away.

When my head finally stopped spinning, I made eye contact with a friendly older man, a bit shorter than I, whose already sparse hair was standing up due to the static electricity from the material of my coat. He calmly lit his pipe, from which came the sweet odor of cranberries.

I intently watched him enjoying each puff, but I gradually realized he was nervous in my presence, his hand was slightly shaking and his intent to control it was unsuccessful.

"Don't worry about my health, dear Victoria. Once I light the pipe it only releases marvelous cranberry smell and nothing else. This is the only way Mrs. Avery helped me to stop with the real smoke. 'Filthy habit,' she said. May I say, it's an honor to finally meet you, my dear girl. You're sort of a legend here." He was speaking with a high-pitched tone that instantly made me smile. I had been expecting a stronger voice out of that old body, not one that seemed young and childish.

"How rude of me! I forgot to introduce myself! I'm Mr. Avery, Sean's most dedicated, old, and trustworthy friend, but you can call me Grandpa A. That's what the Winter Lands citizens call me. I did never ask why but I suppose it's because of my age . . . and after a while, that name grew on me."

Grandpa A lost himself for a second, only to promptly return from memory lane with an even happier face.

"Ever since you learned how to write," he said to me, "I have read every letter you wrote and listened to each story you told, but the beauty of this heart of yours keeps surprising me. Simply magnificent." Grandpa A energetically continued talking, but instead of focusing on his words, I was focusing on his wrinkles that conflicted with his boyish charm and happiness, so that it was impossible to determine his real age.

"Rudolf calling Victoria. Is anybody there?" Rudolf waved his paws in my face, making me blush because Grandpa A now noticed that I wasn't paying attention anymore.

"I'm sorry, but you said you've been reading my letters for years . . . What letters? I didn't write any letter to you."

Grandpa A stood confused. "What do you mean, which letters? Yours to Santa Claus, of course."

He said it like that was an obvious answer. Things kept getting stranger, but the more I heard, the more I wanted to hear.

Grandpa A caught me off guard. "Letters? I never sent letters to Santa. I mean, there's no address. I did *write* them when I was a kid." I gibbered without stopping, with each sentence digging me deeper into a pointless small lie. Once I told my friend Annabeth about my Christmas letters habit, and she laughed at my face. That's why I felt embarrassed to admit it in front of everyone here, no matter the fact I was in the most Christmassy town ever. My tongue was faster than my brain or honesty. It was as simple as that.

"I . . . I don't write letters." I continued to embarrass myself.

It was hard to stop the avalanche of lies.

"Don't worry, my dear, the fear of the deepest wishes of your golden heart being exposed is common and normal among new arrivals. A little lie means nothing to me as long as I'm aware of the truth." I could see he was trying hard to make me feel better and, surprisingly, it worked.

"Doesn't Santa read the letters addressed to him?"

Grandpa A smiled proudly. I seemed to have a strange effect on people here. For a moment I thought Grandpa A seemed like Peter Pan, making me believe that happiness could make him fly.

"Victoria, my winter sunshine. You're the first one who has asked me *the* question shortly after introduction. Brilliant." He jumped around me while Rudolf explained to me in a low tone that Grandpa A was known for giving a lot of compliments because he firmly believed every person felt good after hearing nice stuff about themselves.

Nothing is as powerful as positive affirmations.

"The time to answer your questions hasn't come yet as there are priorities we have to take care of first. Your friends and family can't ever know about this. Let's call it *a new life adventure*. Our valuable and talented operator, educated stand-up comedian, and part-time ventriloquist is the best voice impersonator there is, and he'll make a call to your family impersonating your Italian cousins' voices while you'll talk to them assuring them everything went well after the predicament we had." His monologue called me to my senses, making me doubt reality once more.

"When it comes to explaining things to your family in Italy, you're going to call them and tell them you were resting from the jet lag. You'll add that your relatives from Croatia invited you to visit and it would be rude if you refused, but you're going to be there until a few days before the wedding. And their calls to you, if you're unable to answer, will go directly to our operator. In any case, we have you covered."

When he finished talking, Grandpa A took my hand and we walked down Icicle Street.

Meanwhile, Rudolf disappeared without saying anything, which made me feel lost because he was the one who'd been with me from the start.

"Victoria, as always, you worry too much." Grandpa A already knew what was on my mind. "And, yes, in case you're asking yourself, which you are, there is indeed a reindeer named Rudolph."

That got me smiling, but I didn't really think it through.

"We gave him the traditional name. It was easier than creating confusion. And, no, he doesn't fly. Not any more, ever since people stopped believing in magical things. They've lost themselves in the impossible instead of seeing possibility everywhere."

My mouth was wide open. Every thought, even the fastest ones that crossed my mind and didn't really register with me, was being answered by Grandpa A.

"And, yes, I can read your mind."

"How?" Why finish the question when I figured out his answer was already prepared?

"This invasion of privacy, the mind-reading thing, will only be possible until you start believing in the Winter Lands and stop thinking about it as a dream from which you will soon wake up."

"I don't . . ." The rest of the question was unspoken, but still he answered it.

"It is pretty simple, actually. The moment you start to believe that this place is true, that Rudolf is as real as you and me, to really feel that your belief in Santa Claus means much more than just written letters, only then will your thoughts become private again. This process is important, you see. I am the only one with this ability. You see, because of my human shape—your brain can easily accept my existence. That means you currently believe *only* in me. And *I* am not the Winter Lands, *we all* are the part of it. Once you gain more trust in us and relax in your own mind, when you start questioning everything but embracing things which seem impossible, only then will you become connected to this marvelous place."

It was bizarre to know that the person standing next to you could hear your thoughts like your breaths. At first, you're caught by uncomfortable panic, trying not to think, but that is precisely the time you think the most. And, just maybe, you even start to think about some topics that have never crossed your mind before.

Apparently overwhelmed by my rapid-fire thoughts, Grandpa A tried to redirect me toward something he could handle, since the flow of my intensive thoughts was giving him a severe headache.

"Icicle Street is my favorite one. You'll see; give it a minute or two."

The street was a real spectacle. There were different heights of houses, each with peculiar shapes. People and animals lived together here in harmony, pushing and breaking all the limits in the architecture as well. Each house, store, café, bar, and bakery was decorated with unique Christmas decorations, creating the long-missed warm magic of the season that had once united us all, but which now had universally become a particular type of hype and burden. Looking at this beautiful village, I felt grateful to feel the well-known warmth of Christmas time. Pretty soon, it started to feel like home.

Not only did each of the houses have marvelous decorations, but also on every porch, there stood impeccable crystal sculptures. Their shiny rainbow-colored reflection gave them away. But somehow, every passerby greeted them politely by nodding their heads, not leaving out anyone, in spite of the pedestrian and sleigh-ride chaos on the road.

"Good morning, Harris!" A little eight-year-old boy with messy black hair standing up ran toward the sculpture in the front of the bakery called Sweet Fantasy Buns and gave him a big warm hug.

There was extraordinary innocent tenderness in the boy's touch. It was a moment between the ice sculpture and the boy I couldn't explain. It triggered my thoughts to wildly spin round both of our heads, making Grandpa A laugh. His ability to read my thoughts was my worst nightmare, and I felt ashamed for each thought that crossed my mind.

"Victoria, my d . . ." he didn't finish what he wanted to say, as he was disrupted by one last not-so-polite thought that uncontrollably escaped my subconscious. He grew serious. "Close your eyes. Breathe slowly. Each breath must be deep in order to connect with what is happening within you. Let yourself go to your inner child who already embraced the world with its heart; question but don't demand answers. You'll stop deciding who's weird and who's not and not be insensitive to everything unfamiliar. It's no cliché when I say to look with your heart. How can anyone enjoy the beauty of life if they focus on its negative aspects? This is the main reason why people these days lack happiness, and compassion. Overthinking things is like a disease: it separates us from what we could have done but didn't do, simply because of negative thoughts, which are mainly self-imposed.

Breathe, release, and smile." He pointed his finger to my heart and directed my head toward the kids playing joyfully around the deer sculpture. "Thinking this moment isn't real is equal to saying that magnificent little boy is not real too. What do you *really* see?"

By instinct, I kept closing and opening my eyes, thinking it was a mirage of some kind, but nothing had changed. There was always the same scenery: kids jumping around the reindeer sculpture, trying to touch his antlers, and him pushing them forward slightly in this game, enjoying all the attention he was receiving. The ice sculpture was driven by life, with a strong and shiny red light inside its chest, and I didn't need Grandpa A to tell me how this could be, because at that moment I felt the same warmth as those kids, and the deer's chest shined even brighter. The living ice reindeer sculpture was a measurement of the present happiness. And its chest was radiating with happy red flames thanks to the happy children all around him. It was the same flame of happiness that was now burning inside me too.

"Wow, I didn't expect this. That makes me so happy. Look, Victoria." Grandpa A hopped with joy like a little boy, together with the children, and the reddish color in the reindeer's chest increasingly expanded until it shone up into the sky above us, as Ice Harris shared our happiness.

"It is just as you said: if you believe, nothing has limits," I cheered back at him, full of excitement, and delighted by the people and the whole land. "How come each house has its own ice . . . sculpture? Alive. I mean . . . what do you call them without offending someone in the process?" I was beyond confused. Things like this didn't happen every day.

"Didn't we just have a little talk about overthinking things?" By his tone, I could tell Grandpa A was about to repeat the same words until my mind accepted them, but at the last minute he stopped. Although my head was full of thoughts that were invading my mind like a speeding train, it was clear that Grandpa A couldn't hear anything more. Only silence.

From his surprised expression, I knew exactly what had happened. I could also feel it in me. Instead of thinking of the past and future, I finally started living in the present.

"Each family has its own representative here, close to them in case they are needed. Usually, the ice sculptures help keep them company throughout the day, and thanks to that time spent together, we can tell how much belief is still in the Winter Lands. Think of them as real Santa's helpers. Although made of ice and crystal together, this red light is where the heart was supposed to be, and life is gifted to them by our faith and desires. Which is stronger than it has been in a while with you here. Let's continue."

Ice Harris, the ice reindeer, softly pushed me with his antlers to gain my attention. Then, in a very royal way, he bowed, thanking me for the gift of stronger light.

It was an indescribably beautiful feeling to walk down Icicle Street and be greeted by each inhabitant with wide smiles. People here, no matter the rush, always found a way to enjoy their time, and I appreciated how fulfilled that made me feel.

The thin bond between imagination and reality got lost along the way. Everything in the Winter Lands seemed warm and familiar, so I allowed myself to enjoy the moments here.

With every step I felt lighter, as though I was walking over balloons, buoyed by happiness. The aromas in the air made me feel hungry: freshly baked cinnamon rolls, sweet gingerbread, cranberry pie, a roasted potato from the coal oven . . . . The smell of Christmas was in the air here every day, and I loved it.

"We're here."

At the end of Icicle Street, darkness prevailed, Grandpa A stopped proudly before a two-story house. It had walls made entirely out of copper, carved with stories, just like the WBn Family lamps. The house was already amazing from the outside, while the entire roof was surrounded by little orange Christmas lamps, the only light source illuminating the carved stories.

Through the large windows, you could see a tall, plush Christmas tree standing proudly in the living room. Grandpa A's wife came out to meet us. She had nothing on her feet but plain slippers and was even more excited than he was, if that was possible.

"Oh my, oh my. You finally came. I have been looking forward to this moment since the day Mr. Avery told me a story about a little girl with her head among the clouds, filled with happiness and faith. Vicky, let me look at you." She hugged me and we twirled until my head started to spin.

"Well, I like what I see. Oh, silly me. Please, do come inside, my dear. You're probably freezing to death after all you've been through tonight."

Mr. and Mrs. Avery were made for each other, like cloth to a patch, different in character yet in perfect harmony. I considered it really romantic: two people with one soul and to each its half. I loved the way Grandpa A gave her a kiss, and wasn't ashamed of anyone seeing him. It was purely from the heart.

I stopped on the porch. A strong force was inviting me to touch the words that were carved on the frozen outer wall, and when I did, a magical sense of relief washed over me.

My fingers were automatically moved across the letters to a rhythm while quiet whispers narrated somebody's winter story. The moment was so unique and private, it hypnotized me to listen to its literary melody with my eyes closed.

Grandpa A understood.

"Forever more, when I'm completely tired of searching, disappointed by the people in the world we live in outside of the Winter Lands, I come here, just like you, and close my eyes while listening to the beautiful words coming to my ears. It is a remedy for the soul, a lullaby for my nerves. And I feel grateful for every story that witnesses the existence of good people."

Grandpa A became a little sad, but there was something more to his expression that made me feel his pain. Somewhere inside, there was a battle he was trying to win.

Mrs. Avery called us inside. "You two are going to catch a cold standing like two mummies on the porch."

The warmth of their home, coming from the big fireplace situated in the living room, made me realized I was exhausted and could barely hold my eyes wide open.

"It's okay, Cady. We are not made of marshmallows so we won't melt . . ." He was trying to be funny, but it didn't work.

"Cady is her name?" I was embarrassed to ask, since everyone here knew my name without me even saying a word.

"Yes, my dear. My amazing wife's name is Cadelia, but we call her Cady because it doesn't have as harsh a feel as her real name, don't you agree?"

I didn't agree entirely. For me, Cadelia was a rare and pretty name that fitted Mrs. A like a glove.

"Mrs. Cadelia . . ."

"For you, honey, I'm Cadelia or Mrs. A. It's fine not to call me Cady. Just don't make me feel too old, like Grandpa A. That's on him."

"Oh, Cadelia, you have such a wonderful home. The atmosphere here feels awfully familiar and warm. And the ornaments . . . Just *wow*."

My compliments to Cadelia made her face light up. It had been a long time since someone new came to the Winter Lands and been so amazed by the lifetime of effort she had put into the house, her masterpiece.

Not only had she faithfully collaborated in transcribing the stories with the WBn Family, but also she had handmade all the ornaments out of leaves, flowers, pine needles and pinecones, painted the glass balls, and paper ribbons. On my surprise, the candles too were handcrafted with love, each in its unique way. The living room, where we were standing, was illuminated by candlesticks, while the other rooms had bright eye-catching orange lights, creating a cozy, romantic tone.

The main focus of the decor wasn't the ten-foot Christmas tree which was taller than the doors in the living room, but the simple candle centerpiece on the dark brown solid-oak table.

A crystal candlestick in the shape of five leaves was firmly holding, with interwound fingers, a roughly shaped angel candle whose wings stuck up in the air along with its hands as though it was embracing someone invisible. It was as though it was kindly greeting someone, welcoming them with intense love.

"This is remarkable." The words just popped out of my mouth. Never had I felt so enchanted with a material object before.

"Just like my wife." Grandpa A couldn't hide his immense pride. "The most talented woman I ever met, my lovely Cadelia."

Grandpa A informed me that Cadelia was preparing supper, so he showed me the way to my room where my luggage was waiting for me. I could finally change my clothes and refresh myself. Unfortunately, I knew all I would be able to do was to climb the stairs and jump onto the bed. I had no other choice since my sleepy eyes refused to stay open for a minute more.

"Grandpa A? I want to thank you and Cadelia for dinner, and I'm sure it's delicious, but would you mind if I went straight to bed?"

Cadelia joined us at just the right moment and gave me a look that questioned why I was even asking them that. "Of course, if you need anything—"

"Just a glass of water, thank you! But I am not hungry anymore." I looked apologetically at Grandpa A. "My mind and body are beyond overwhelmed by all of this, and I need a good night's sleep so I can think better in the morning."

They were clearly understanding people but Cadelia couldn't hide a tiny bit of disappointment in her smile. I guessed there was something she had wanted to talk to me about, but it would have to wait for another day.

She tried her best to sound happy. "Of course, my dear. All is prepared for you here, and dinner is the least of your concerns. Goodnight, Victoria." Her voice was soothing and gentle, not revealing what her smile was hiding under a veil of melancholy.

"Sweet dreams, child." Grandpa A surprised me with a fatherly kiss on the forehead.

"Thank you, Grandpa A." I smiled back. In this kiss, I recognized my father, grandfather, and uncle all in one, and I knew why the Winter Lands had decided to give him his nickname.

Tiredness came over me so fast that I couldn't even remember how I put on my favorite star pajamas and threw myself under the blankets.

In my dreams, I kept going over what had happened to me so far, in a slow-motion continuous way, from the dance with the Flash to chaotically losing myself in the international airports until I felt Rudolf's paw upon my arrival in the Winter Lands. But every dream was somehow interrupted by an unrecognizable face. It looked like the face of an old tired man. At first, I thought that was my grandpa visiting my dreams. But no matter what efforts I made to catch that man or at least the figureless face, each attempt was annoyingly unsuccessful. I didn't recognize this person, but I felt like he was close to my heart. It felt similar to my strange encounter with Brian and Flash, but at the same time it was a completely different connection.

*Who are you?* My voice was a strange, distant echo. *Why are you so sad?*

*Can I help you? Do you know me?*

There was no reply. It seemed like the man didn't have enough strength to say anything. The sorrow on his face was almost palpable, while his helplessness was devastating, even if it was just a dream.

For the rest of the night, I was able to sleep peacefully, but my mind continued the search for that lost face in every corner of my dreams.

The next morning, the beautiful melody of the birds in the trees woke me up, mixed with children's laughter while they had snowball fights with the new layer of snow before school.

I took a deep breath in and then exhaled slowly, enjoying it while it lasted. "This is what I call perfection." I stretched my whole body, especially my legs, under the big pile of warm covers filled with soft feathery material.

If it hadn't been for the snowflakes calling me out, I would've stayed longer under the blankets just as I had done in childhood. My ears caught a loudly ticking clock on the wall, showing five-thirty in the morning, but I felt rested enough.

It was strange to wake up in a place I didn't quite understand, though I didn't doubt for a second that I was still in the Winter Lands.

*I wonder why Rudolf disappeared on me without saying bye? Will I see him today?*

Thinking about Rudolf was suddenly something normal, as though I was thinking about a best friend.

I cheerfully moved to the window where a long window seat was waiting for me filled with big fluffy pillows and an L. M. Montgomery book along with a cup of hot chocolate.

After a sip of the chocolate, I felt my stomach growling—I was hungry. I've opened the doors sightly but could't hear any sound coming from the downstairs. So I went back inside my room, finished the hot chocolate and continued reading the book.

My mind and body were consumed by peace and tranquility: two strong, comfortable feelings.

❄

When I had read three more chapters, I tried to sneak down the hallway on my tiptoes just to try to hear if anybody was in the house, but the ancient floor was being cranky and loud. The moment I opened the door, the smell of just-baked crepes and eggs with onions entered my room, driving my taste buds crazy. I ran like a child, sliding down the handrail all the way to the living room, right in front of Cadelia, almost knocking the tray of chocolate brioche out of her hands.

She didn't say a word, but there was a big smile on her face .

"Good morning, Victoria." She offered me warm brioche right away before taking it to the dining table.

"Is this for me? I could never eat all of this by myself." Food covered the entire length of the table, mimicking the bright colors of the Christmas tree. It was a feast for my eyes, which made it difficult to decide what to eat first. I always found it easier to have fewer choices.

"Darling, you can eat as much as you want, but I do believe it is too much food just for one person . . .. We will have guests for breakfast. It is our morning tradi—" Cadelia wasn't able to finish before a horde of kids making a lot of noise entered the house running directly toward the breakfast.

They ran around the table like I didn't exist, with only the food on their minds, before stopping in front of Cadelia. They already knew that their first stop, after taking their jackets off, was the bathroom sink.

"Victoria, why aren't you eating?"

"No, no . . . I'll wait . . . my companions." I wasn't sure how to call those children.

*Were they her grandchildren?*

"Miss . . . um, Cadelia, can you tell me where Grandpa A is? Or bear— um, Rudolf is?" There was no way to hide being uncomfortable asking about Rudolf. The talking bear had grown on me the day before, but today I was questioning whether it was still real or had been a hallucination.

"Don't worry, Mr. Avery will come for you after breakfast. You two have a lot to do today. Meanwhile, just relax."

"And Rudolf?"

"He'll wait for you in the C.I.Z., known here as a Christmas Industry Zone."

When I begun to eat, all thirteen of the children sat around the table and started asking me a bunch of questions, having never seen me before. I was on cuteness overload.

The smallest one, with long orange braids, stood up on the chair and leaned toward my ear. "What is your name?" she asked softly, like a whisper in the wind.

"Vicky, and yours?"

"Melissa. Are you going to eat with us every breakfast in Grandpa A's house?"

"Not every, no. I'm just passing by, I think." I gave her my most honest reply because I didn't truly know anything about why I was in the Winter Lands.

"That is just too bad because Grandma C cooks hav . . . hev . . . um . . ." She was trying to find the right word, which was sweet, as she kept rolling her eyes with the effort.

"Heavenly? Is that the word you wanted?"

Melissa's eyes lit up. "Yes, how did you know?"

"Because I'm a grown up, I'm supposed to know the words. How come you're here in the morning?" I enjoyed watching while they ate, not caring about anybody watching them.

"We . . . every breakfast . . . parents . . ." The little boy across the table tried to talk with his mouth full while the sourdough bread crumbs continued to fall in his lap.

"Don't talk with your mouth full, young man. Not only is it dangerous, but I can't understand a word you say." It came as a shock hearing my mom in my voice, but it had an immediate effect on the little boy. He chewed all of his food and then started to speak clearly.

"Sorry, miss, I didn't know." He was pronouncing his words carefully.

"We come here to eat breakfast every morning because when our parents work early shifts in Crystal Slides, we hang together here before school and after if needed. I guess we're too small and they don't like leaving us home alone. Some of us do tend to make a mess . . ."

I didn't expect such an elaborate answer from a six-year-old boy. Luke seemed very intelligent from the way he spoke, even with his slow pronunciation of words. It felt like talking with an adult in a kid's body.

It surprised me how I knew about their names and age but I decided to let it go.

*Maybe this was another one of the Winter Lands abilities.*

And thinking about the abilities of this place reminded me of yesterday's dream. Suddenly I felt sadness again, hopelessness—like the person from a dream was someone close to me that I couldn't help.

Somehow, despite my smile, Melissa noticed the change in me.

"Vicky, why are you sad?"

She continued to interrupt every sentence of mine with that same question for the next twenty minutes, even though I politely replied—multiple times, I didn't want to talk about it. That is until Cadelia came from outside to see what was going on at the table.

"Oh, it's nothing." I categorically refused to talk about what had been bugging me ever since last night's dream, but Cadelia followed determinedly up on Melissa's persistance, leaving me no space for possible lies.

"Victoria, when a child as small as Melissa notices sorrow in your eyes, that's a serious situation. Never before has a new arrival been sad in this place, but I guess there's always a first time for everything. What's going on?"

"Cadelia, it really isn't—"

She interrupted me immediately. "You know why the Winter Lands is a happier place than the rest? It's not the ability to understand animal talk, or because of the international beauty this place possesses, but because of our ability to talk or argue about what we feel, think, and do. Whatever is on your mind, it will go away once you learn how to say it out loud. Not one emotion is worthless, and each has an immense value to our soul."

She was right, I didn't argue that. The only thing was that my worry wasn't as hard on me as she might think.

"Cadelia, I'm not sad, I guess. I don't even know how I feel exactly, and it's all because of the strangest dream I had last night. It seemed so real." I couldn't really work out where to begin as I didn't know why a dream would ruin my mood.

"Oh, dear! You had a bad dream here in the Winter Lands?" Cadelia's voice sounded surprised but compassionate.

"No, it wasn't bad. In the beginning, it was a dream like any other, but I kept seeing an old tired face appearing everywhere. A face of an older man with wrinkles, that could easily have been my grandpa. He didn't seem sad. Worse, his expression was empty, outside as much as inside. Something in me knew he was lost and couldn't find the way back home. I don't know, Cadelia . . . Maybe told like this it doesn't sound like something special, but to me that dream represented something inexplicably important. Listen to me, I talk like he is a real person."

Maybe I lacked the words to describe it better, but even so, Cadelia's face became serious and she turned to the children. "Are you finished with breakfast? Yes? Perfect. You can all go to the second floor to the playroom. C'mon now. I'll be right behind you."

After they joyously left for upstairs, Cadelia sat down next to me and politely asked me to explain my dream without excluding anything.

After I had finished, she disappeared briefly before returning. "Victoria, I filled in Mr. Avery and Rudolf about what's been said here. They'll be here soon. Unfortunately, I can't keep you company any more since I have a bunch of kids to take care of before they tear my house down." We could hear loud screams and children running upstairs, thumping with their tiny feet like they were made of stone.

The house was filled with warmth and love, so I couldn't help but wonder if Grandpa A and Cadelia ever had children of their own. In the manner of a clumsy private detective, I circulated the living room looking for any kind of indication of extended family. Other than framed memories of the two of them, I didn't find what I was searching for.

"Anybody home?" Grandpa A's voice startled me, as my head was buried under millions of thoughts.

"Grandpa A." I ran to the entrance of the house and helped him take off his heavy coat.

But I continued starring at the doors behind him, trying to see if Rudolf is going to show up.

Grandpa A seemed to have figured out my worry because I kept starring over his shoulder.

"Rudolf just went to arrange our transportation because we are going to visit Christmas Industry Zone today, a place in which we take great pride, as—"

He couldn't finish; Rudolf was already cleaning his snowy paws on the welcome mat at the entrance.

"Rudolf, you're here." I exclaimed overjoyed, not knowing if I should hug him or not.

"I don't bite." He welcomed me with open arms, and my bear hug made him laugh. He clearly hadn't expected me to connect with a talking animal so fast.

"That's how I know this isn't a dream," I whispered so only he could hear.

Grandpa A and Rudolf sat on a long brown couch just underneath the wide windows that revealed the winter scenery in the backyard. Noticing their excited yet fearful expressions, I anticipated the next question.

"You want me to tell you about last night's dream?"

Grandpa A nodded his head. "Just like you told it to Mrs. A."

In my retelling of the dream, I saw it all: raised eyebrows, suspended breaths, and somewhere in the corner of their smiles, a glimpse of hope.

"Could you be so kind as to describe one more time how the man looked?" It was the third time Grandpa A had asked me that.

"NO pressure!" Rudolf looked as though he was trying to calm the electric nervousness between them.

"All I remember is a friendly old face lost inside my dreams . . . with unbelievably sad big blue eyes . . . Nothing else. Oh wait! He had something around his neck, a necklace of some kind, in a very strange shape. It looked like tiny thorns or mountains, something . . . not quite sure . . . And it looked like we were in New York . . . I am sorry I can't remember more, but I didn't know my dream would be so important to you."

But they had stopped listening somewhere around the necklace part. Grandpa A and Rudolf were staring at me without blinking. After what seemed like minutes, both heads started to move in the same rhythm up and down. Their weird behavior made me feel confused and even a little mocked, though I would soon realize that my assumptions were way off.

"What in the world is going on with you two? Why did I just spend almost an hour explaining my stupid dream? It's just like any other: annoyingly hopeless! It's really not the first time I woke up sad because of the strange activity of my brain during sleep."

"May I?" Grandpa A asked the bear.

"By all means . . ."

"Victoria, we understand the pressure that is on, since yesterday, with everything seeming unclear or unreal, but it would be a lie if I told you it's not going to get any weirder than this. Not for us, but for you."

I took my time to breathe deeply. It was the only way to suppress the dizziness.

"Meaning?"

"It means that the person you've dreamt of, right here in the Winter Lands—which can't be a coincidence—is the same person we've spent years searching for," Rudolf chimed in.

He allowed Grandpa A to continue. "Twenty years, to be precise.

Our search, until now, was unsuccessful and nerve-wracking, because we lost the most important person of this place twenty years ago when Sean decided to go out there in the world with a mission to discover what was making people lose faith in good. He really wanted to make a difference but he wasn't prepared to fight off the same feelings he was trying to investigate. And so, the three days he had planned for became twenty long years and counting since we almost lost our hope and have been trying to run this place without him. That is . . . until *you!*"

I could see that Rudolf was eager to tell me everything he knew too, while Grandpa A's rhythm of speech was going at a plodding pace.

"A long time ago, when I was just a cub," Rudolf said quietly, not allowing Grandpa A to get a word in, "I experienced an unforgettable, splendid moment when Sean Christmas chose me as a representative of my kind.

"I knew from the start it was a great honor to have throughout my lifetime. But to be honest, I didn't know how many magical, tearful moments I would experience reading letters from around the world and the joy they would bring to my heart—and to each heart here. On a foggy December day, the sweet, short words of your first letter— *started with Dear Santa*—were imprinted onto the Christmas List Board. I won't lie to you, it was like most first letters: short with quite a few wishes, in elementary school handwriting, filled with traces of Christmas excitement. But as years pass by, children tend to change their style: the list gets proportionally longer until the sad year comes when the letters just stop. So when that day came for you, and we didn't expect your signature anymore, your letters kept finding their way to the Winter Lands, with the list also getting extensive—not with material stuff, but with wishes for your family, friends, and people you didn't even know. We all said, 'That hasn't happened before. It's a special moment the Winter Lands can be proud of.' But let me continue. Eight years ago, when you turned eighteen—the age when almost no one ever writes Santa Claus letters anymore—we received a letter from you. Then I realized your love for people was more significant than materialistic aspect of Christmas, and I believed it could warm people's hearts and make important changes to this crazy, chaotic world. Your wishes go beyond the material: toward what is right, second chances, and the life you so proudly sustain with faith. I just regret Sean didn't have the opportunity to see them. He would've been so proud. Along the path, you've learned how small things create your life choices and that no fear should last for an extended time. There is always sun after the rain. Each of your letters became a short story where you were worrying more about others' well-being than your own. And that wish list that is still present at the bottom of the letter? It's a beautiful childish habit that always was and will be taken into strict consideration."

"Rudolf, you're losing yourself." Grandpa A was eager to finish the explanation so they could take me to the Christmas Industry Zone.

"Pardon my enthusiasm." Bear Rudolf smiled. "You see, Victoria, Sean Christmas is the older man from your dreams. We are almost sure of it."

I was confused by everything I had heard, and couldn't figure out why this was important. "Who is Sean Christmas? Can someone explain this to me?"

Grandpa A and Rudolf looked surprised.

"Do you really not understand? 'SC' stands for Santa Claus. Victoria, who else could it be?" I could swear Rudolf was angry with me again. If bears could get wrinkles because of emotions, he would appear ten years older by now.

"Oh, shhh . . . Rudolf, maybe this whole trip was too much for her." Rudolf ignored Grandpa's attempt to help me, and lost himself once more.

"Avery! But on the letters . . . She should've . . ."

"Rudolf, you seriously don't understand . . ." Their dispute continued while my mind wandered.

I walked over to the table and put my palm over the lighted angel. If it hurts, all of it is true and real. If there's no pain, then I must've been dreaming.

"Oh, it burns!"

They hadn't noticed what I was doing. "So, when you spoke earlier about my letters, you were telling me the truth. There is a Christmas List Board?" I was just repeating the facts like a parrot. Surprisingly, it helped me maintain my focus.

"We are perfectly aware of the situation you're in," Grandpa A stated, "but the fact remains you dreamt about Sean Christmas, which makes you the first and only NWLP to whom this has happened. Somehow you two have a strong connection."

"NWLP?"

"New Winter Lands Person."

No matter what they told me, I still didn't feel any different nor as though I was of importance.

Both of them continued to explain how things in the Winter Lands happened, down to the smallest detail, trying to emphasize how huge a deal everything was, but my mind was elsewhere, running outside toward the piles of snow, imagining making pretty snow angels while dancing with the snowflakes. Rudolf's sneeze brought me back into the living room but only as far as the Christmas tree. My eyes were jumping from decoration to decoration: glass icicles; warm lights with an orange glow; handmade sparkling snowflakes; red balls of glass, velvet, and other materials. Cadelia hadn't left any part of the tree empty, putting her love and devotion onto those branches. Just looking at the Christmas tree was enough to bring all the sweet childhood memories and its happiness to my mind. And then there was the angel decoration on the top of the tree. The angel motif was everywhere in their house like a protector with a small golden heart sewed on from the outside so it could be seen, holding to it tightly and not letting go.

"My precious wife made this angel, the first one of many, right after our daughter died."

This confession took me by surprise. I sensed that Grandpa A had never before shared his own story with anyone from outside the Winter Lands, but it seemed that the simple dream of mine had been enough for him to trust me and to share his story.

Before he started, Grandpa A took a few deep breaths. I noticed Cadelia sitting silently at the top of the stairs.

"She didn't make it through the birth, our Honor. Today she would be a marvelous twenty-year-old college student, complaining about how her strange parents live far away and trying to figure out how to tell her friends why they can't visit us. But someone among the stars had a different vision for our Honor and us. After she left us so suddenly, we were shattered . . ." His voice faltered as tears filled his eyes. "It took only twelve days for my brave wife to decide, from that moment on, our life goal was to cherish and take care of as many helpless, lonely, or abandoned children as we could because we couldn't have any children of our own anymore. Cadelia has so much unconditional love in her heart, my amazing wife . . . And I supported her every step she decided to take, and that was our Christmas promise. This was when she made Angel Honor as our everlasting symbol and a reminder of how precious life is, no matter the obstacles in our path. Shortly afterward, we got an extraordinary and surprising invitation from Sean Christmas to join the Winter Lands, thanks to my wife's efforts to make the world a better place, where she could blossom with love and potential for the greater good." Even if his story had started out sad, as he talked, I saw how the tragedy had become the source of their daily happiness, the loving memory of Honor. The little tear escaped the corner of my eye.

"Rudolf, please, can you do me a favor and prepare the sleighs?"

Grandpa A asked politely as he softly wiped the tears from my red cheeks.

He let me calm down, and after a few minutes we put on our coats, ready to go to the Christmas Industry Zone.

"Victoria, do you realize that, out of all of us, you were chosen, by Santa Claus himself, to find him?"

"I don't know, Grandpa A. Though I'm sure of this: I am in the Winter Lands. But apparently, during my accidental sightseeing with Rudolf, I saw the Himalayas and the Dolomites, not so far from each other. And you are all extremely generous, kind, perfect hosts, but this is a lot to take in all at once. On top of that, I am Santa Clause's only savior?" I started to cry again: I had been feeling emotionally wrenched since that dream, but this time I also felt the pressure on me. Cadelia, Grandpa A, and Rudolf didn't add anything, but I knew perfectly what hope meant: a responsibility that would be put on me not only by them but also by the entire Winter Lands.

Inspired by Grandpa A's honesty, I decided to be honest myself.

"It's fair enough to warn you, *"if I get back"* . . . sorry, when I get back, I can't guarantee the memory of this place will stick with me, except as a marvelous dream."

He appreciated my honesty. "It is a risk we're willing to take. And what's all this about if I get back? Of course, you're going back home." They were somewhat offended.

"I just assumed, since you told me how both of you came here by invite and stayed . . ."

"Don't assume anything. Nothing here is ever as it seems. Your mind should be trained to fight every negative with positivity. Let's go."

Out on the porch, goosebumps ran over my body while my lungs filled with sharp, cold, mountain air. Before us, there was a big sleigh overlaid with tons of outdoor pillows, with a bear as a driver. On the front there were six magnificent reindeer, one behind the other, with their tall royal antlers.

I couldn't wait to touch them. Reindeer hair proved to be soft and silky. Meanwhile "Jingle Bells" started running through my head. I guess old habits indeed died hard.

It was another wish I could cross off the bucket list.

"Victoria, are you ready for the best sleigh ride of your life?"

I was so excited I just nodded.

Grandpa A covered us with a fluffy green blanket.

"If you're ready, so am I." Rudolf pulled the rope, nudging the reindeer to start. They moved, first with a slow gallop, which became a quicker trot as they showed off the potential of their lean but strong legs.

Soon we were sliding fast through untouched forests connected by birches that were making the most amazing arcs with pine trees, and we found ourselves overlooking Canada's breathtaking Lake Louis, protectively surrounded by gentle mountains, creating a sense of harmony.

"Grandpa A, this scenery is perfection." I still couldn't cope with the fact I was in every winter continent at once. The thought was too scary to be taken quickly, so I just had to relax and let myself go by being open to new things.

The path was sharp and led uphill. The endless curves made it feel like my entire breakfast might come up, and I forced myself not to look down to avoid nausea which came along with my fear of heights. Rudolf could smell my fear.

"Victoria, please relax. These reindeer know every inch of this land, and nothing bad could happen. I'm sitting in the front just to be their company and make them laugh. They are party poopers because work makes them too strict and they become rule followers, but I manage anyhow." He didn't hide his happy smile.

At one point a view opened up of a golden valley filled with millions of colorful lights. Those lights made a gigantic pine-tree shape, whose branches were forests carefully planted. The park's fountains were shiny vibrant Christmas balls whose water made star-, heart-, and angel-shaped holograms, while strangely shaped architecture was used as the valley's tree decorations. All of it was happening under the mountain chain that seemed like a sharp cloud above the flattened trees. I felt extraordinary, absorbing as many details as my brain could process.

"Where are we?"

"This is our diamond, the Christmas Industry Zone." Grandpa A stood up, proudly pointing a finger toward each structure beneath us.

"Do you see the wooden building like a picnic basket? That's a famous Wooden Shop, where the finest men are making furniture, toys, and sculptures out of all types of wood. Right behind them, a little bit to the left, the pine-shaped edifice? It's called Where the Pines Stand Tall and it's the most spectacular greenhouse and ornaments warehouse, with decorated trees that are being tended every Christmastime. One of our most significant achievements, may I add.

Also, can you see the clumsy huge ball surrounded by more than ten thousand stairs, which slowly turns around its axis? The restaurant Like to Eat is baking the best pies ever, and whichever flavor crosses your mind, they transform the idea into a sweet creation. Of course, other dishes are not far behind—all heavenly," he added.

Far off in the distance, behind the StarQuarter and DecorM buildings, I spotted an ice-skating rink similar to the one in New York, which reminded me of my dance with the mysterious Flash. For a second, my thoughts stayed frozen in time, trying to get the best out of that moment.

Thoughts occupied my head like dominoes falling until I was able to clearly see my parents and sister. And I missed them because they were the ones I would've shared this moment with.

Rudolf screamed at us, "Please, both of you, be seated! We have a lot to do." His impatience made me giggle. I really enjoyed this bear's company. Who wouldn't?

As we got closer to the Christmas Industry Zone, I wondered how it would be to live here one day, where people don't envy, hate, or condemn without putting themselves in your skin first. I'm not saying that perfection is a goal of life. They had issues here too, of course. Naturally, so many different tempers don't always fit together perfectly like a puzzle, but one could feel respect and mutual trust, sensations which are long gone in the real world, having been ripped from us due to our narrow minds.

In the Winter Lands, you could work on yourself without having to look at who was watching and how they saw you and your actions.

The entrance to the Christmas Industry Zone was exceptional, filled with little colorful lights on every tree, along with a joyful hologram messages and videos of good deeds all around us. If I thought their town was magical, this blew my mind completely, starting with those bright lights everywhere, the rush of people, big fancy bows, the smell of the restaurants, and candies . . . All mixed in a unique perfume spreading throughout the air.

I couldn't wait to jump out of the sleigh and dash to the fountains nearby. I felt like a child again. It took me down memory lane to Christmas Eve, when you just can't decide whether to fall asleep or stay awake the entire night just to hear Santa. And in the morning, you run downstairs to the Christmas tree, whose pine needles made the house smell good.

"Victoria, everything you see is the legacy of Sean Christmas and his ancestors. The Winter Lands is always excited, yearning to be discovered by good-hearted people. But, you see, nothing is the same without the person who was a little kid when all of this started to be a bigger mission than ever before. Without Santa Claus, we aren't lost, but we aren't so good when it comes to resolving problems and everyday challenges. Not to mention, we are facing problems with some of the toymakers that worked with us for years. Ever since the population grew fast, we needed extra help with making happy children around the world. Because of less belief, and Sean's disappearance, we are slowly losing ourselves. His imagination and desire to help are endless. Also, very few of us have dared to search for him over the years. We do wonder if Sean managed to lose himself, whether the same destiny is awaiting us. Does one defy the fear or embrace it? Most of us choose safety."

I was trying to listen to Grandpa A's stories, but the technological part of the Winter Lands was astonishing at every turn. I found myself staring into a square display unbelievably similar to a tablet, as tall as a twenty-story building, which was actually a tall thin wall of EletroTechLAND, where the entire Christmas Industry Schedule was visible and apparent. I asked the obvious question: "Why didn't you track his phone? Judging by all I see, you've embraced technology. You don't seem to have any problem mixing it with tradition."

"Sean is a special person, dear Victoria, a big fan of everything new. He knew the world could become greater with the development of technology, but that doesn't mean being a slave to it. So, when Sean decided to observe the world from inside, he left the Winter Lands with only a backpack, a plane ticket, and some cash. All he wanted was to see how a normal person sees the world, to live in the hustle and bustle, under continuous time pressure. He wanted to figure out what went wrong since technology was supposed to make life easier and create more leisure time. The only directions he left us were about thinking about new projects for the following Christmas."

"Grandpa A, I know new generations aren't perfect, but . . ." I admit, something in me needed to justify our behavior, but when you really thought about it, any justifications you could find weren't strong enough and wouldn't stand up in the court of the Winter Lands, if there were one.

"What can you possibly say? Isn't it true that traditions are slowly dying, families don't have the same values, kids are growing up way too fast, and you all depend on the time but not the other way around, like it is supposed to be?"

"That is all true. No matter how much you like me, I am one of those people too." The truth was sometimes a curse and a blessing. I understood the urge that had driven Sean Christmas out of the security of Winter Lands, but one question didn't leave my head.

"You have to excuse me for asking this . . . How do you know Sean Christmas is alive after being gone for twenty years? Maybe you're chasing a ghost. Isn't he replaceable? I don't want to sound cruel but you did say 'Sean and his ancestors'. That has to mean there were other Santa's " I knew my questions sounded a bit blunt, but without the answers, I couldn't understand their hope.

It seemed like Grandpa A had expected this interrogation. In fact, there was a tiny smile in the corner of his lips.

"When you're Santa Claus, death doesn't go under the radar. On the contrary . . . And while I'm still hoping it won't happen anytime soon, death would be a time when the Aurora Borealis disappeared for two weeks without any trace all around the world, and the star in the Milky Way belonging to Sean Christmas would be the only bright light, next to the moon, for those two weeks. Fortunately for us, we didn't see anything like that over the years." He shook my shoulders, deadly serious now. "Can you understand what I mean by you being the only one who found him, at least in your dreams? That's more than the rest of us have been able to do. Maybe you're the person who will save him and bring him back."

Hearing those words finally spoken out loud, I knew they were expecting a lot from me, and I didn't want to be a disappointment, but I still couldn't understand how I could find someone they couldn't.

"But Grandpa A, I am only twenty-six years old. With so many obligations hanging over me, including my last year in the grad school, finding a job . . . What if Sean isn't in America, but in Japan? Or Africa? I can't—"

He interrupted my negativity. "His last call-in to us was twenty years ago—at that time, with a payphone—two days into his journey, from a small village in Scotland. He was traveling with our unique Winter Lands portals—I will explain it to you when the time comes; we usually use them *only* in emergencies. You see, Sean had mapped out the entire itinerary; he was supposed to enter the New York though the Central Park portal, and then to travel, and meet people until he reaches one of the biggest Winter Lands portals in Utah. By walking through the portal in the Bryce Amphitheater, in Utah's National Park, he would've had the last stop in the New South Wales,

Australia. There, on The Snowy Mountains, he had a Winter Lands special transport called RushUp Tube to take him home. He used to call us from the payphone on two occasions: before he was leaving the state he was in, and before using the next portal. That's how we know he is still somewhere in New York, and that is probably the only visible bond between you too. Plain, improbable, but valid. You're all we have now, Victoria. You've said it yourself, the surrounding you saw in the dreams was the Manhattan skyline."

"What if I forget about the Winter Lands?" I was still feeling overwhelmed.

Grandpa A looked at me with an expression full of faith, imploring me with his look, telling me there was more to me than I acknowledged. "Trust me." He tapped his own chest. "Inside there is more magic than in this place, and the immensity of it will never leave you completely. A little faith in yourself can't hurt you, Vicky!"

Our talk was interrupted by persistent thumps on my calf from a reindeer who was trying to show me something.

I gave a confused look to Rudolf, who had to guess the meaning of his action—the reindeer were refusing to talk with him. Apparently there was an old feud between them. Rudolf told me he might've had exaggerated on multiple occasions when he made fun of their seriousness. "I think they want to take you somewhere. It doesn't often happen that reindeer are so friendly with the new arrivals, but I guess news spreads fast here too."

"Do we have time for them to take me?" The reindeer were ecstatically tapping their hooves.

Grandpa A smiled. "There's always time. But you and Rudolf should go together, I have work to do. The rest of the day should be all about fun. I'll catch you two later."

I wasn't even able to say goodbye before the leader of the reindeer pushed me into the sleigh. They had enormous strength in their marvelous antlers.

"Where to?" I was curious.

Rudolf nodded. "I have a wild guess." But that was all he was ready to share. The reindeer knew better.

Soon we were speeding through the forest, taking corners past the buildings with a precision that caused my stomach to become shaky with excitement.

"What was that?" We sped close by a brown fountain with a sign saying Chocco Point.

"The chocolate factory. My favorite! We didn't really see it clearly, but there is a cool entrance, and the factory space goes deep underground, the reason the tempered chocolate is so easy to make! It's funny because I always leave that place at least four pounds heavier." Rudolf chuckled.

At the mere mention of chocolate, my eyes brightened and my mouth filled with saliva, even though I wasn't hungry.

"Can we do a pit stop later at Chocco Point? Pretty please?" I was thinking about everything I had read or watched in *Charlie and the Chocolate Factory*, and my imagination was running wild. The factory building itself wouldn't be anything like the movie, I knew that, but just the glimpse of the fountain was enticing, and I never said no to a treat.

My biggest surprise came when the reindeer stopped in front of the ice arena, an ice-skating rink as big as four football fields, decorated only by bright lights. I loved to skate, but I couldn't help but wonder why we were there. The answer came from the nearest forest. Reindeer started to come out, one by one, with their calves too. I didn't need Rudolf to explain why they wanted to meet me, as they were putting the baby deer in the front of the line so I could pet them all. They were such wondrous, glorious animals, my heart was melting out of happiness with every tender touch. Those beautiful round eyes were full of hope as they watched me carefully. The pressure I had been feeling grew more significant.

"I can tell you miss him a lot, and I'll do my best to find him, to find Santa Claus."

After all those years believing there was unexplainable magic in the world, after all those letters that I had written and addressed to Santa Claus, I was finally speaking about him as a real person. It wasn't as weird as I expected—in fact it was fulfilling: it made me feel important, although I felt torn between reality and dream. Who wouldn't?

Suddenly, a strange combination of anxiety and laughter hit me so hard I couldn't breathe, and I burst into a sincere and genuine laugh.

Rudolf took me by the hand and pulled me onto a bench, but I couldn't stop laughing. It got even worse as I tried to put ice skates on. My voice was so loud it overtook the music on the rink.

Soon Rudolf and I were skating, alone and joyful, and not one doubt or negative thought crossed my mind.

Afterward, Rudolf granted my wish and took me to that marvelous chocolate factory, whose outside wall was double-layered chocolate that, due to the low temperatures, was harder than marble. The faint scent coming from the hard chocolate walls incorporated an orange flavor. Inside, the factory was packed with sweet sculptures, some similar in size to Michelangelo's statues, and others tiny chocolate decorations. I didn't know where to look first. I spotted a beautiful starry sky made out of the purest Belgian chocolate. On the chocolate sky, the inner clouds were white chocolate and surrounding clouds were dark chocolate, while little stars, made of brown

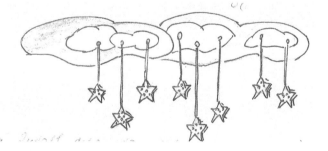

shiny caramel, hung off the clouds with the finest milky threads. When Rudolf told me I could take one, I hesitated at first, not wanting to ruin the design.

"Come on, Vicky, give it a try. Reach for the caramel pieces of the sky. In case you're wondering, as soon as you eat one"—he pointed to the chefs behind the decorated mirror—"they will fill it up with a new one. I'll hold the ladder tight for you. Go now."

If someone were to ask me what my best moments in the Winter Lands were, I would say it was when Rudolf smiled because he lit up everything around him and you could see happiness written across his face.

There were workshops for pralines, chocolate sticks of all flavors, cakes, ice creams, and candies. When we walked down the long hallway, which seemed never-ending, we came across a colorful warehouse packed full of millions of gifts and wrapped desserts waiting to be delivered. After the mostly prevailing brown color we had been seeing, my eyes needed a few moments to get used to the colorful decorative papers sprinkled around the room.

"Is this for the kids?"

"Naturally, but also for every lost soul. Chocolates are not big gifts, but these days, they belong to a dying tradition. Once, people didn't have much, and when they found little chocolate treats under the Christmas tree, it meant the world to them. Nowadays, kids freak out if they don't find smartphones or tablets under the tree. Parents are scared of sugar like the plague, not realizing it is about moderation and control. The old times were a perfect example. Now people overthink things, including the small but necessary joys of life. And that's a shame. Now go ahead and pick one."

"Seriously? But how? They have stacked the gifts tightly. It's like a big puzzle. If I pull one out, everything will collapse."

"Victoria." I knew when he addressed me with my full name, he was about to lecture me. "You should learn not to worry about every single thing. For Christmas's sake, just pick one, say its name aloud, and let the system show you its splendor." Rudolf showed me the labels on each package.

"Yes, like I could read those names four feet above us, if not higher." My sarcasm lately always had the wrong timing.

"Look at her. Still waiting to be told everything. The binoculars are in front of you, almost touching your nose."

They were indeed in front of me, but in my defense, they were almost camouflaged among their surroundings. Nevertheless, it made me think about all the things that had often been in front of my nose that I hadn't paid attention to, while blaming circumstances or other people. Today Rudolf was giving me life lessons.

"I want—"

"No, you *wish* for."

"Okay, I wish for PurpleCandy04."

When I made my choice, a little purple package with a blue ribbon jumped from the last ten-foot-tall row, directly into my arms. Nothing even moved on the big shelves. The empty hole was filled with another identical package moments after.

On the label, bigger than the package itself, was written: "Chocolate Hazelnut, filled with blueberry juice, pralines with heart sprinkles '04."

Rudolf was gloating. "I told you, nothing here in the Winter Lands is as it appears at the outset."

"Wow, this is awesome." The urge to call more packages was barely controllable, but I somehow managed to curb my desires.

"Now that you've seen Chocco Point, I absolutely have to take you to Candy Top, where we have the coolest slides in the world. One of a kind." Rudolf grabbed my coat, put me on his back, and ran on all fours the entire way to another side of the Christmas Industry Zone. On our way, we saw the Squirrel Squad again, cleaning the paths with such dedication that humans would have envied them.

"Do they ever rest?"

I guess no one had ever asked Rudolf that, so he took some time to think. "I don't think so. Being maniacally controlling is their trademark."

The smallest red-striped chipmunk ran behind us trying to jump on Rudolf's back, unsuccessfully. At first, I thought she just wanted to have the ride of her life, and it seemed cute, but when she actually jumped hard enough to catch up with us, she scratched my leg.

"Ouch! What's with the aggression again?" It came as a surprise, and Rudolf stopped right away and took something that I had been stuck to my jeans. It was an acorn.

"This is what she wanted from you. Our chipmunks don't tolerate public petting. And to them, work and maintaining family are the most important things there are, nothing else."

Candy Top wasn't a building. It was an enormous slide, and I had a feeling Rudolf hadn't explained that because he knew how I froze at every mention of heights. As we entered the structure, the wide spiral hallways reminded me of the interior of the Guggenheim Museum: they contained laboratories of candy making, full of people controlling the environment in sheer rainbow suits, and in the middle of it there was a wide curvy pipe, transparent and completely empty going from the bottom to the top. Now I knew why it was called Candy Top.

"Is that . . . ?"

Rudolf was bursting with laughter. "Oh, yes. The question is, are you brave enough to accept the challenge?"

Truth be told, I wasn't feeling brave at all. My knees were shaking, and my head was dizzy. But it seemed stupid to give 'no' for an answer in the Winter Lands.

"Okay, I'm in. But it is far up. How do we get there? With . . . balloons?" I spotted helium-filled balloons on the doors, behind which, frizzy green-apple candies were being made.

"No. By foot . . ." He was giving me that condescending look again.

"Well, why not? I am talking to you, right?"

"Girl, because of your word choice, you're sliding first."

"Oh, I'm so in. Let's go. I'll race you to it." The words popped out of my mouth, forgetting there was no way I was going to beat a huge bear running on all fours.

When I got to the top, short of breath and gasping for air, Rudolf was already waiting with a shallow snow sled in his bear paws.

I was still trying to calm my beating heart when Rudolf pulled the bell near the start sign, and a noise came out of the walls like something was going to break them, and the floor under our feet shook in small but fierce vibrations.

"Rudolf, what's going on?" The rustling sound scared me, so I held firmly onto the wall in search of stability.

"Patience, Vicky. You'll see."

Shortly after, through the holes in the wall, candies started to flow inside the transparent tube, literally flushing down.

"Candy River! I dreamt of this once." My fear vanished.

I confidently took the sled from Rudolf, positioned it straight ahead, and yelled, "Ho, ho, ho."

He couldn't hide his surprise. He wasn't even ready to follow so quickly after me. I found myself zooming down the Candy River slide. From the inside, the tube looked endless. It felt like I was suspended in the air on nothing but candies, and that made me giggle more. I was making strange noises I'd never made before, and I knew the lab people could hear me even through the thick plastic enclosure. Honestly, I had never had so much fun in my entire life.

If the thought of going back up wasn't so challenging I would have gone again, but I chose to wait for Rudolf at the bottom.

"Candy River is always fun, no matter how many times I try it." The bear was as happy and exhausted as I was.

"Here you go." He handed me the map of the Christmas Industry Zone. "We don't have much time at our disposal. Pick three more destinations to visit because Mr. Avery is waiting for us across the street." Rudolf pointed at the strangest building I had seen yet in the Winter Lands. It looked odd because it was so simple and white, with no distinctive architecture, just a silver sign saying Gift Your All. That simplicity gave it a kind of beauty.

Without Rudolf explaining, I deduced what was going on inside: human kindness at its best.

Then a question, entirely off-topic, crossed my mind. "Rudolf, does time stop here?"

"No, time flows equally everywhere, but how you perceive that time is what makes our land different. We don't live here to run after time, but instead, we learn to embrace it, to make the most out of it, and be aware of the fact time works for us. I'm still relatively young for a bear, twenty years old, but if there's one thing I'm sure of, there is no finish line. Life slows down, allowing you to use each second the best way possible." After that unclear response, he paused, leaving me to think about what time meant to me.

"So, it means you're not like two hundred and something years old?"

"No. Why make something like that up before even asking? Questions are asked for being answered."

"I am sorry, Rudolf, the almost red-nosed bear." I chose my words wisely to lighten his mood before the serious apology kicked in. "I am truly sorry. I look for sarcasm in everything, but that is how my defense system toward new stuff works. I'm well aware that I have used it too much. I promise not to jump to conclusions anymore."

"It's a lot to deal with, Victoria."

"Don't give me excuses." I looked him in the eyes. "If I do all that now, I can only imagine how I would deal with bigger issues, and that scares me. I don't want to be part of the problem; I want to be part of the solution."

Rudolf stared at me, seemingly impressed that no matter what pressure I had on me, I was catching on rather quickly to the real Christmas spirit and life. "Even with that, I still wish more people would be like you. Sincere apologies are always welcomed."

Now, I took a closer look at the Christmas Industry Zone map, and although I'd ideally have wanted to see everything, I limited it to Where the Pines Stand Tall, Christmas Library, and Gift Your All workshop.

"Nice choices."

Standing in front of Gift Your All workshop was heartwarming. The building was simple in structure but surrounded by bushes decorated with millions of small lights spreading into the meadow behind it. I felt like they were calling out my name, so I walked towards them—in a hypnotizing way—and after a slight touch on one of the light bulbs, I knew exactly what it represented.

"Every light is for one kid that's been helped and taken down the right path in the world." A tiny tear dropped off my cheek. "How do I know all of this?" But I didn't wait for a reply before continuing. "My God, there is goodness in people we are not aware of."

I was surprised; *mesmerized* was the right word.

"Let's go inside." Enthusiastically, I ran inside, calling out to get people's attention, since my entrance had been all but subtle.

The inside area was divided into four parts with striking labels: toys and material, monetary donations, dry food, and clothing. In each department, approximately fifty people from the age of eighteen years onward worked. They were dressed in casual attire with two hearts linked together made of elaborate handmade red lace on their shirts. Each of them wore a wide smile, regardless of how hard they were working. People inside were casually talking, while the objects continually streamed through the walls from large tubes similar to the ones in Candy River.

"These presents and donations are coming from all around the planet?"

"Yes, but consider this a small part of it. When it comes to donations, we work globally and have more than one location."

"How many are there?"

"One center for each city on every continent."

"Really? Wow!"

He was talking about more than a ninety thousand locations where they helped people. It was impressive, but not as much as the dedication they were putting into their work. They clearly loved the job since all of them were smiling.

In that instant, I wanted to be part of the Winter Lands. The need to do good was always within me.

I approached one of the tables which was filled with colorful envelopes.

"May I?" I politely asked the older woman unwrapping letters at a sloth's pace. Fast work didn't seem to matter as much as how thoroughly the work was performed.

A small, square letter with boat designs on the front grabbed my attention, so I gently opened it.

*Dear Santa Claus,*
*My dad and mom don't have much, but every year I get gifts under the Christmas tree. I know they work for you to make me happy—they told me so. They said they had a secret contract with you I can't speak of. Psssst, I know how to keep a secret. My wish this year remains the same. Help the ones in need—that's what my momma says. And please bring something nice to my parents.*
*With all my love,*
*Carly, age 9*

Reading those words enabled me to feel the exact emotions the little girl was going through. She had such a kind soul.

I wanted to open more.

*Santa,*
*Here's the $50 I earned shoveling snow in my neighborhood.*
*I've been trying to give this to an old lady that lives above*
*my best friend's apartment. Mrs. Allis keeps sending it back to*
*me. Can you please do something about it? I'm not sending*
*this letter to you, but I do kind of hope the money magically*
*appears in her apartment so she can buy herself fresh food.*
*If my friends knew I still believed in you, they would make*
*fun of me because it's not cool.*
    *Thanks,*
    *Sanders, age 15*

"A fifteen-year-old boy wrote this letter to Santa and just sent it in?"

"He didn't. The moment he imprinted those words, beginning with Santa's name, they appeared in the Christmas List Board."

Genuine, authentic magic was real here in the Winter Lands. I would have continued to read, but Grandpa A came along holding a little girl's hand. She had on the cutest pink dress, and had an angelic smile, with eyes that were big like chestnuts. And they were followed by other kids behind them.

"Well, hello, pretty girl!" I knelt next to her while she played with her curls. "What is your name?"

"Addie," she whispered cautiously, but then added, "My friends call me Little Addie Warrior, and I like it very much." Looking into her eyes, you could have drowned in kindness. Her movements were graceful, like a ballerina's, and she was clearly smart for an eight-year-old kid.

"And why do they call you Warrior?" As soon as I asked the question, I wanted to take it back.

Grandpa A jumped in. "Addie said it all: she's giving a fight worthy of a warrior." But when he saw my confused look, he felt encouraged to continue by a whisper. "A fight against leukemia. The Dark Evil. It was easier to explain it to her this way. Kids love good stories, where good overcomes bad, and it helps them not to think about the future but to live in the present."

I had to keep what I was feeling inside without showing it. If Little Addie could be so strong, I had to reflect her attitude.

A couple of times I tried to say something, just to start a conversation, but I couldn't say anything. The only question I had was why something as ugly as that would happen to an innocent little girl who just wanted to live a life in peace and happiness. Grandpa A felt my sadness: he may have known I had never been in touch with such a young, sick child, so he let Little Addie play with the letters while he tried to explain everything to me about what they do in the Winter Lands and how every year they help children around the world not to feel different no matter what obstacles life puts in front of them.

Each year, the Winter Lands chooses visitors from a wide range of possibilities, mostly homeless or sick children who need magic, joy, and laughter in their lives. Sometimes, all it takes is just a little goodwill to show how faith is crucial when it comes to achieving inner peace.

After the Winter Lands, most of them return to their previous ways of thinking, believing that coming here was just a beautiful dream. But memories can't disappear so easily: they remain present throughout their dreams, following the visitors like a guiding star in difficult moments.

"Victoria, you shouldn't be sad about their destinies. That bitter feeling usually stops people from living in the moment. Instead, you should celebrate their lives and cherish every moment you get to spend with those marvelous souls. People tend to feel sorry for themselves and others so easily, and they don't understand that the more faith and gratitude you nourish, the better it is for your mental state and for the ones you're so worried about. Each heart needs infinite love, no matter how sad, sick, or poor it might be."

Grandpa A managed to stem my tears of sadness and transform them into tears of joy. I had to realize just how much power I had in me to make their days better. At my request, we stayed among the children for the next three hours, playing and talking, until Grandpa A and Rudolf came up with a brilliant idea.

"Would you like to take them all to Where the Pines Stand Tall?" Rudolf knew my love for kids and pines would do magic, but first I had to promise not to let myself cry again because it wouldn't help the kids.

Just then, a tiny warm hand gently took mine.

"Oh, hello."

"Hello . . . Can I hold your hand? I'm too little to walk alone."

"It would be my pleasure, Nora." Simply looking at her angelic face brought the girl's name to my mind. My hosts exchanged a surprised look that they tried, and failed, to keep secret.

On our way, we played a lot with snow, while bothering the hardworking Chipmunks Squad. The kids, just like I had, wanted to pet them, not knowing their attitude. But that didn't stop them; soon enough the Chipmunks Squad escaped from them. Those kids were far from being scared by anything or anyone.

❅

Where the Pines Stand Tall was an incredibly beautiful place, with a structure in the shape of a real tree. Inside, the main room was filled with numerous decorated pines, while each floor branched to other small rooms where decorations were awaiting a newly scheduled change. Each level had a different set of ornaments, making it difficult to concentrate on a single pine with its luxuriance.

Watching the children running toward the hundreds of pines, I finally understood why the child's spirit is so unique and free. Their love was immense, while showing a constant curiosity without fear or judgment. They were embracing everything with huge happy smiles on their faces.

The past, for them, was just a beautiful memory they had to leave behind to create the present. A small number of people in this world manage to keep that attitude while growing up, keeping the pure innocence of the soul, not being changed by the rules of today's society.

I wished to be among the ones that look at the world like kids do, even in my eighties.

My first instinct was to scream at them not to run, in case they fell. Instead I yelled, "Be careful."

"Can we go up? I want to touch all the trees." Bobby was pulling my coat.

"Yes, Bobby, I want to do that too." When he asked me, I smiled at his suspicious look when he asked me why I didn't give orders like his mom.

As we entered deeper into the structure, the smell of fresh pines took over the air. It's incredible how smell can trigger an avalanche of memories. It was as though I was a child, playing among the autumn leaves, smelling the upcoming snow in the air. And I was grateful for each marvelous memory from my childhood.

It only took a second for me to start acting like the rest of them, dancing together around the many trees: the Christmas tree, autumn tree, Thanksgiving tree, Mother's Day tree, love tree, smile tree, and many more. We happily sang every song that crossed our minds until Little Addie had an excellent idea.

"Grandpa A promised we could trim one of the plain Christmas trees. Can we do it now, Victoria? Oh, can we? Now?"

"Of course."

We chose the smallest tree because I wanted kids to have the perfect height to decorate the tree themselves. To decorate, we had to go inside the branch hallways that contained different kinds of ornaments from around the world, each unique in style, colors, and smell. I said the kids could do whatever they wanted as long as they didn't argue while doing so. They had to learn about friendship, sharing, and respecting each other even in simple situations like this one.

It was great to see that Christmas trimming didn't lose its charm here, and tradition was respected as it should be everywhere. The labels we give each other weren't important while everyone was synchronized and acting as one, still respecting their differences.

❄

Over the next few days, Rudolf and Grandpa A showed me the entire Christmas Industry Zone, except the Crystal Slides Mountains. That was the only place you needed Sean Christmas's permission to enter, as lightning often hit the top of the mountains, making snow crystals out of flying gushes of snowflakes. Since Sean had gone missing, the mountain range hadn't been working at full capacity, and Crystal Santa Guards came to the bottom of the big sleeping giants, not allowing anyone without prior permission to enter. As Rudolf said, you could feel the real sadness of Santa's disappearance there, so most residents avoided it.

I had the most wonderful days in the Winter Lands. Rudolf and Grandpa A made the best of this experience so I wouldn't forget about the existence of the Winter Lands when I go back home with a task of finding Sean.

They didn't talk a lot about my dreams, which continued to get stronger, repetitive, and more precise. I could feel the tension at the sole mention of Sean's or Santa's name, but no one dared ask anything despite the fact they were eagerly waiting for me to say something that would miraculously reveal Sean's whereabouts. The last morning in Avery's house, after breakfast, I've sat them down and told how my dreams seem more vivid.

"I could recognize his face anywhere. Grandpa A, he looks closer to your age now. I hope that's ok for me to say. There is a new detail; I keep seeing him in a green-grey uniform with a little tag. But I still cannot read it out."

Even though I was expecting cheerful reactions, they listened to me calmly without a spoken word afterward.

Every citizen of the Winter Lands wanted Santa to find his way back home, safe and sound, but they weren't sure what to think about me or this strange connection we had in dreams.

Then the day came for me to leave.

Grandpa A and Cadelia sat me down after not asking a single word about Sean for days.

"Vicky, it's time for you to go back to your everyday life . . . I know you have a wedding to attend." Grandpa A sounded disturbed. He wasn't talking as much as he usually did. He searched my face in complete silence.

Cadelia eventually spoke. "There is one thing we failed to mention."

She took a deep long breath before she continued.

"You haven't been the only one, Victoria. Here, I mean . . .. We have had a lot of other guests here who had minor connections with Santa, though not through dreams like you . . . but almost all of them forgot about it once back home. The small percentage of those who kept their memories weren't able to locate him . . . Either way, the world these days has become an unquestionably strange place, Victoria. It's no wonder Sean couldn't find his way home. Somewhere on his mission, he lost himself; although using the portals might have had something to do with it. The point is, we are not about religion, politics, or the economy, but about love and children. If they don't learn how to help, educate, or listen to other people, how can they care or even love each other with no resentment or hate?

How can they become a new leaders of the world?

Kids that didn't learn their lessons when they were young are now the same ones starting wars and spreading hate." Grandpa A was on the verge of crying while listening to Cadelia.

She took his hand and pressed it against her heart. It was a gesture they exchanged to comfort one another during emotional storms. Those two were an example of pure, unconditional love.

"It makes him really sad hearing or repeating the same speech every year without seeing results. We tend to enjoy a lot of happiness, but that makes it hard to handle negative emotions. Which isn't good either, I am well aware."

I don't know what exactly came over me, but I had to put their minds at ease.

"I promise I'll do my best not to be like the others. I *am* going to find Sean Christmas. Our Santa Claus. I will. I am sure of it; that is what I have to do."

To me, those words held value, but I knew that they were just another promise to them, no matter how solid their trust in me might be. And I couldn't blame them.

But strangely, on that snowy night, I stopped being afraid of the unknown I would have to face.

The next day, early in the morning, Rudolf gently woke me up with his soft paw, whispering to me my breakfast was ready. It was four o'clock in the morning, and he didn't want to wake Grandpa A and Cadelia. I had a feeling they were wide awake and simply didn't have the strength to say yet another goodbye.

Since our conversation the night before, I had been feeling more alive in my intentions. Just to know there was a meaningful purpose to my life and to find myself marked by this amazing adventure meant a world to me.

The table was overflowing with food, warm pancakes dripping

with red fruit sauce, scrambled eggs with asparagus, salad, mixed fruit bowls, even the chocolate-fudge orange-flavored brownies that I had first tasted in the jet that brought me to the Winter Lands. I guess Cadelia did all this for me.

Rudolf didn't give me much time to enjoy the meal. "Ready to go? There is a serious snowstorm ahead of us, so it will take longer to reach Winter Plane."

Still sleepy, I could only shake my head—just as in every marvelous moment in my life, I didn't want this to come to an end. I got up from the table and took two more looks around that helped me memorize the details of the house.

"If you do remember the Winter Lands when you step on the familiar ground of your world, you must not tell anyone about it. You have to realize by now, Victoria, people often don't understand those who think or act differently. They tend to exclude roses from a garden of only tulips, and I'm not saying that to scare you." He adopted a much lighter tone when he noticed the worry on my face. "But just to remind you, everything you do or believe in, do it with a heart full of honesty and never change your good ways just to impress someone or to fit in."

I'm not sure why this thought crossed my mind at that moment, but after all my conversations with Rudolf, I was positive he could be a great leader of the Winter Lands one day.

This time, a plane was waiting for me in the Christmas Industry Zone at the top of the Gift Your All workshop. With all the snowflakes swirling in the air, we could barely see the path in front of us— it was a good thing the reindeer knew the way. I've found out from Rudolf that when it snowed this heavily the Chipmunk Squad went ballistic because they couldn't properly do their work, and instead were supposed to rest at home. Nevertheless, all of the squirrels, from young to old, were peeking out of their homes. They were scared to say goodbye too, and not wanting to do anything to jinx my mission; I could feel it in the air.

What came as a big surprise was the pilot was nicer to me, and even seemed respectful. It seemed that news in the Winter Lands traveled fast and far to other areas.

I couldn't help but wonder what they saw in me that I couldn't.

"Victoria, remember, if you know deep inside you can, it means you will." Rudolf knew he was repeating things I had already been told, but he didn't care. Out of all the inhabitants of the Winter Lands, Rudolf suffered the most, since he was the first to be forgotten when the Winter Lands visitors went back to the outside world. He explained why:

"I know the Winter Lands, and Santa Claus has priorities. It will always be that way, but one tiny part of me sincerely hopes the day will come when I'll be just as important when remembering the Winter Lands... It is hard to believe a walking, talking bear named Rudolf is real, and that is the first thing that persuades you to think the Winter Lands is nothing but a dream ..." One small tear escaped his eye, and he broke down for the first time in many years. His voice cracked and he couldn't meet my concerned gaze. "Don't forget me, Vicky ... " He hugged me tight and then for the second time since I had met him, , he ran away quickly, like bears do. I guessed he was probably doing it to create a "normal" memory to add to the existing ones.

With a cup of hot cinnamon cocoa and a Harry Potter book, I was finally on a plane heading to my original destination: my cousin's wedding in Italy.

# The Bench Under
# The Willow

I was finally home.

It had been a week since I'd got back from the wedding, which was incredibly emotional and romantic, just as I expected. Fortunately for me, my relatives there believed the story about me visiting my hometown first, just as my parents did, and it didn't seem strange to none of them; on the contrary, they were expecting it. I was lucky my parents were immersed in their work obligations, so they didn't have time to ask too many questions. They kept postponing it until they eventually forgot. They were more interested in the wedding.

Not for a second had I stopped thinking of the Winter Lands and the responsibility on my shoulders. I had been waking up every morning with the fear that I might forget about it before returning home. But I had been lucky so far, and my memories were intact.

Rudolf had told me that the amnesia usually happened when a person came back to their everyday routine, with family, friends, and coworkers, at which point everyday life took away the memories and transformed every adventure into an everlasting dream.

Just thinking about it made me feel gray.

My dreams came more often, and each morning Sean's face became more vivid. But who knew if those dreams were past or present? That thought was haunting me throughout each day.

*Do I actually see him in New York now or was this long time ago?*

Twenty years of being lost is a long time.

Days went by without me doing anything. I unconsciously kept myself away from friends and family, frustrated that I couldn't tell them about Winter Lands or Sean, or ask for help. At first, my parents attributed this behavior to my nostalgia about the other side of the family, but as I continued with this behavior, they clearly didn't know how to explain my unexpected aimless wanderings in the city, or why I often skipped class, which was something I had never done before. They became convinced that I was deeply in love, and my mom would spend days telling me that love doesn't make us ghosts.

Then, one day, while I was sitting in my favorite coffee shop, with an open map of New York, someone pulled my hoodie.

It was Brian.

He startled me, appearing out of nowhere; my thoughts were among the countless faces passing the window. "Let me know one thing: Why did I have to hire a private investigator to track you down so I could invite myself for that coffee you promised?"

My mood changed right away; I never knew how to hide my feelings, and was always prone to blushing. Brian understood immediately as I got up to kiss him on the cheek and say hi.

"What is going on in that pretty head of yours, Vicky? I don't think I've ever seen such a foggy expression in your eyes."

After the weeks that had passed, what I really needed was to tell someone what I was dealing with and how enormous it was, but I couldn't. A promise was a promise. And Brian belonged to our world.

I took in a deep, tormented breath. "I lost a friend, and I can't find him." It just came out of me—I wasn't even thinking if I'd have to explain that sentence.

"Did you try to find him on social media? It usually does the trick." His response put me at my ease, as he didn't ask any details. "Look, I'm not kidding. It might well help." Brian was immediately trying to be helpful. I had loved that about him when I first met him. I guess that was the trait which helped him in the financial world.

"Don't get me wrong, Brian, I'm truly grateful for the support and you trying to help me, but of course I did all if it. And it didn't help." I wouldn't usually have sounded so resigned, but the lack of a good night's sleep and my inability to even start figuring out where Sean was had taken a toll on me.

I didn't want to forget the Winter Lands, Rudolf's happy face, the neurotic Chipmunk Squad, Grandpa A and Cadelia, the children, Ice Harris . . .. Fear of forgetting didn't allow me to relax. So, I switched the topic to his business.

"And you, Brian? Everything went well with your trip to Chicago?"

He looked as though I had thrown him off guard.

"You remember?"

He made me blush again, by not lowering his intense look until I took mine away. In one look, it felt like he could reveal my soul and hold it in his hands.

He smiled. "It's funny, but it seems like you tend to forget stuff connected with me or to forget me overall."

I could see he only meant it as a joke, but I couldn't help taking it personally.

"Can you please stop repeating the word *forget*, because if you don't, I'll get up and walk away right now," I reacted pretty harsh.

Curious heads around us turned to see what was wrong. But in a split second, a sour mood had come over me. I felt like the time was the Grinch, trying to steal my Christmas assignment, with every hour closer.

I had never seen this part of myself before, but I disliked it right away. How I acted only showed I had Grandpa A's task close to my heart, and with all of my will, I wanted to restore faith in the people of the Winter Lands.

Brian didn't say anything at first, which made me feel even worse.

"I'm sorry. I am so sorry . . ."

"No, I understand. You're apparently under a lot of stress." He kept quiet and that was fine by me; it soothed my soul.

"Let's go." Brian stood up and took my hand.

"Where?"

"Do you trust me?"

My reply was automatic. "Yes."

"Let's go. Hurry up before it closes!"

"Before what closes?" I got the feeling that Brian would have integrated perfectly into the Winter Lands. They all had the same habit of not explaining things.

❄

Minutes later, I found myself in front of Rockefeller Center and the skating rink.

The tiniest fragments of memories connected to bigger one, showing me a picture I hadn't been able to see before.

The day Brian and I met, in a coffee shop next to the Rockefeller Center, when one hand shake won over each emotion I had ever felt for him . . . The cloudy Tuesday when I left him sitting there, without looking back . . . Brian's kiss of surprise at the airport . . . It all finally clicked.

"You're Flash?" I stared at him without shame, hypnotized by his gaze just as he was by mine. After that, courage kicked in, and words started flowing. "Somehow, deep down, I knew, but didn't allow myself to admit it. The touch of your skin even before you kissed me. My friends thought I was crazy, but my heart knew what my eyes refused to believe."

That marvelous and liberating courage to admit the truth was something I learned from Rudolf. And it felt so good.

It didn't look as though Brian had expected such an honest reply. He was used to me running away, so the happiness in his eyes was priceless.

"Victoria, don't you think we're past the point of games, and now it's our moment?"

While exposing his emotions, I could see he was frightened of my reaction. In the past, he had tried to do the same, but we were younger and naive—my inability to express my feelings out of fear of getting hurt backfired and it had ended up with me walking away, sad and disappointed. Due to overhearing the mean commentary of his friends, I thought I was just prey in a silly boy's games. Only later did I find out Brian wasn't sharing their view, but at that time, I felt it was late to say I was wrong and sorry.

But now I continued speaking honestly. "I think I am ready now, Brian, but only if you're going to have patience with me. Yes, I need you in my life. I'm finally aware of that, and you always felt it. But for a while, I need your love but without any questions. Can you offer me that? Is your love that strong?"

I could see the happiness and acceptance in his eyes. He hugged me, and it felt like we were never apart.

That night I woke up from some awful nightmares, anxious and sweating, with my heart skipping beats. Sean Christmas hadn't been anywhere in my dreams when I needed to see him the most, and I had been pulled into a dark abyss without any way out. I got up and went to the kitchen to make myself some hot chocolate, which was my equivalent to a lullaby.

Somewhere in the middle of the cup, I closed my tired eyes unconsciously, when I heard a familiar voice.

"Victoria, you will never forget me. The connection of our hearts is stronger than any doubt. Breathe in and out . . . There I am. Find me."

It was his voice; Sean Christmas was talking to me.

How was this even possible?

Santa Claus was near, and he wanted me to know that.

I returned to bed, knowing tomorrow was a new day. Finally, my mind was at peace.

Just as I closed my eyes, a cold breeze blew into my room through the window, which was slightly open as usual. The city of New York went quiet as well. The small vibrations of the sound were trapped between the snowflakes, transforming the city into a peaceful playground.

The next morning, I woke up rested without anxiety hanging over my head. Even before I got to the window, I could smell snow in the air.

My classes for college started later, so it was the perfect moment for a walk in Central Park.

"Alone again?" Mom couldn't disguise her suspicious look over the kitchen counter as I inhaled my pancakes.

"Yes."

"Victoria, what's wrong with you? Since you came back from Italy, you've been enjoying being alone more than spending time with your friends or family . . . I am worried about you. Did you fall madly in love with some guy you met in Italy and you miss him so bad that you cannot function properly?"

I laughed at her wild imagination, but she was entirely serious.

"No, Mom. I'm not planning to move to another continent." I

washed my plate and then headed to my room to get dressed.

She smiled with obvious relief.

"For now," I added.

And with that, her smile vanished as I continued to laugh.

"Mom, I'm going to the park to relax before studying. See you in an hour."

I could hear her mumble something to herself, but if I stayed there to find out what it was, it would only prolong our conversation, so I skipped that part. My love for my mother was strong and always would be, but some space was needed between us.

When I left the building, I noticed how the crisp white color was wrapping the city in the magic of the moment, while the snow was still falling with no intention of stopping soon. The sharp smell of winter air gave my legs more strength as I headed toward Central Park.

Oh, if people could still appreciate everything like they did in the past. Today, unfortunately, everyone was chasing time and not enjoying it. Precipitation of any kind was loathed in the broader population because of the way it weighed down on their commitments and traffic.

I calmly strolled through Central Park, which was filled with little children and parents in the eternal snowball fight, which I joined in a couple of times. To some of them, my intrusion may have seemed lame, but some kids welcomed it. Everyone should try regularly to do something without planning or purpose—pure, spontaneous reaction.

Over a small bridge, I noticed the weeping willow, deeply inclined under the weight of fresh snow. It was the same willow that I saw just yesterday in my dream. I recalled it immediately. I closed my eyes, concentrating on a small wooden bench beneath the willow from my dream, only to open my eyes and see the same bench in the distance, even through the falling snow. A man was sitting there, not moving, feeding birds in the cold.

Instantly, I knew I had found him!

My heart began to beat furiously and my hands started shaking, more with each step I took toward the bench. I tried to walk as quietly as I could, but the sound of my boots crunching in the snow announced my arrival.

Sean Christmas looked directly at me. He was exactly as I had seen him in my dreams, but so different from the twenty-year-old picture Grandpa A had shown me back in the Winter Lands. It wasn't to do with his age; people grow old, that's part of life, but there was a void on his face where once there had been a smile so big it could light up the entire city.

He seemed like an old lost soul, sitting all by himself, feeding the birds, as though he was enjoying the loneliness just like my mom told me I enjoyed mine. But he had been repeating this routine longer than me.

I could see the reason he didn't send me away was that he recognized me. From the way he looked at me, I was sure we shared the same dreams.

"Victoria . . ." He looked at me, firm, and confident in his pronouncement.

"How do you . . .?" I stopped myself from asking. As usual my tongue had moved faster than my brain. "Dreams?"

When Sean nodded sadly, it broke my heart. I could see how perplexed he was.

"I've been dreaming of you for the last couple of weeks without knowing why or where you were." It was me who started the conversation, since he seemed like he needed a little push to open up.

But Sean knew exactly how to respond. "On the other hand, I have been dreaming about you for almost eight years, or maybe even more, since I have your first letter to Santa Claus impressed upon my mind. I still don't know your real age."

That caught me off guard in the most unexpected way. "You remember who you are? That's great! But why didn't you try to find your way back home to the Winter Lands then?"

Sean looked at me as if I had fallen from the clouds, and he wasn't sure exactly what he was supposed to tell me. "The Winter Lands? Never heard of it. And I don't know where you get your information that I actually know who I am. If you mean the name, that is the easy part, but . . . I feel as though my heart hasn't been able to find its place for more than twenty years. They keep telling me it's early Alzheimer's, but I know in my heart it isn't. Maybe it's amnesia." Sean looked gloomy but he didn't lower his gaze.

"So how do you know me? Only through the dreams?"

"Call them dreams, visions, daydreams . . . For a long time I tried to repress my mind, telling myself I'm not crazy, but it didn't work."

I noticed he was wearing a park uniform with his name on the little worn out tag. That was another important detail from my dreams I was unsuccessful to figure out.

"You work here? How come I've never met you before?" I was struggling to believe it. Santa Claus was tired and lost, living and working right next to me, and I had never noticed this sad face before. I wondered what Rudolf would say to me at this moment.

"I don't know why I work here, Vicky. What I remember is leaving my more-than-well-paid job at a prestigious law firm for pro bono cases, to be a guardian in Central Park. Everyone kept telling me I was a fool, crazy to say the least, but you know what? I didn't care what people thought of me because here I finally felt comfortable in my own skin. Just being here feels like home, of which I still don't remember anything, but I know the emotions and sensations well. Especially on days like these. And for me, playing with the kids, taking care of animals, and helping people are things I can't live without. The problem is that every time I get close to the answers to my questions and prayers, something in me blocks those feelings and memories. A big black hole swallows up all my happy thoughts. Then, out of the blue, I'm finding it hard to even breathe. That's the vicious circle that repeats itself over and over, trapping me here, leaving no escape.

"But right now, just by being around you, I'm feeling your warmth, joy, and faith, and it is giving me hope I didn't have until now. Somehow, you're making me believe there is more to this than meets the eye." It was clear Sean was speaking from the heart to this stranger he had seen in his dreams, where he heard my every Christmas thought.

I felt his every word in my heart, and so I vowed to do everything in my power to bring Santa Claus back to the Winter Lands—the only place he belonged.

"Don't worry, Mr. Christmas." I took his old wrinkly hand in mine. It was like holding my grandpa's hands: I felt so much love in one touch. "I'll help you find your way home. You'll be able to see miracles around you once again."

I knew I shouldn't tell him who he was yet. Grandpa A and Rudolf had warned me that, in his current state, he would never accept it as truth and I would risk losing him. The Santa's memories could be triggered *only* with grand gestures of kindness.

Once I had made my sincere promise, I noticed a happy tear escaping Sean's eye.

"What do I have to do, Victoria?" He no longer looked like a helpless old man, sitting like there was no tomorrow; now he was sitting upright, and looked more decisive and willing to be guided.

"Don't worry about anything. We have to bring back your memories without disrupting your present. That is how you will remember what you did before ending up here."

"Can't you just tell me? I can feel you know. You are carefully talking to me, like there is something unspoken you avoid to reveal."

But Grandpa A's orders were clear, and there was no room for error: I couldn't tell him just because I felt sympathy for him, nor was I allowed to take him to the Winter Lands without his memories recovered. "You have to remember on your own. I told you how we need to do it if you don't want to lose completely your memory. And, since you've lived here for quite some time now, I am afraid you wouldn't believe a word I say."

It was hard for me to leave him there, but I had to head back home; I had taken much more than the hour of walking I had planned, and I was supposed to attend afternoon lectures.

That was the agreement between Grandpa A and me; no matter what was going on, I wasn't supposed to skip my everyday education.

"My house isn't far from here, five minutes away from the park." He was scared of us losing each other.

"Then at the same time here tomorrow?"

When I nodded my head, he smiled broadly.

We had found each other because of forces bigger than both of us.

Happiness flooded my body, and any stress I had been feeling disappeared although a feeling of exhaustion kicked in as soon as I came home. But I didn't care. Tomorrow was going to be a beautiful new day.


Back home, I couldn't figure out what to do with myself because of the ecstatic butterfly feeling in my stomach. It wasn't like the Winter Lands had a book of rules to follow in these situations. Just the thought of that kind of rulebook made me laugh.

Just when I was about the start the letter with *Dear Santa* so it could be quickly imprinted in the Christmas List Board; to notify them about this important news, I've noticed a big white envelope with shiny red letters written in the Winter Lands' beautiful calligraphy. My mom had seen it, and she obviously couldn't work out who had sent it, but I could immediately smell the scent of the place.

I still couldn't figure out how they send their letters to me.

I was so excited to have news from the Winter Lands that I opened the letter as fast as I could, wondering if they somehow knew about my discovery through some magical means.

*Dear Victoria,*

*I would love to write you sweet, good news, but life brings obstacles into our path every so often to remind us to live with commitment.*

*Unfortunately, for quite some time now, we are aware that our biggest toy supplier has decided it was time to retire, and although we shared his happiness for his special moment, we feel worried and sad now! Mr. Mayerin's time to relax has come, and he has left his entire legacy in the hands of Robert Mayerin Jr., who inexplicably cut off every connection his father had cherished so fondly throughout the years with Sean. He just doesn't seem to believe in magical things or in wonder.*

*Even though we were planning—with the best intentions, to involve our New York headquarters to help you in your search quest, now I have to notify you that you are all alone.*

*Frankly, I could have sent someone from here, but we are afraid of them losing their memories just like Sean. And, mind you, he was the bravest of us all.*

*My dear child, I know we already put a lot of pressure on your gentle shoulders, and I apologize for that in the name of entire Winter Lands. But please remember, we will always be by your side, regardless of the outcome of your search.*

*Thank you, Victoria, for everything!*

*Always with you,*

*Grandpa A, Cadelia, and Rudolf*

Though I was honored by their trust in me, I felt suddenly over-whelmed by the scale of the task the Winter Lands was asking of me.

*I'm only me. Victoria, who doesn't dare to ask people on the street the time because she's too shy*, I thought.

There wasn't time to stall. I had to make a plan that would help me to solve these problems. I'd always been someone who postponed whatever could be put off until tomorrow, but now I had to change my ways.

# Bringing Back Santa

In the following days, I was a complete mess trying to coordinate my exams with the daily tasks I had to work on before meeting Sean Christmas at the same bench. It seemed every attempt of trying to trigger his memories was falling on rocky ground. Unexpectedly, the memory of the Winter Lands slowly started to fade, and Grandpa A's letter was the only thing that kept me believing that the isolated world of the Winter Lands was in fact real.

I hoped the ink in the letter wasn't some kind of magic ink that disappeared over time as it was a link I treasured.

Despite all the notes, calls, and plans I had made, I hadn't moved on from the dead-end I was in. Each day Sean looked more helpless than before, as if my presence was now making his amnesia steadily worse. His hope in me had not immediately produced results, and his ongoing loss of memory left him in insurmountable grief.

One Saturday night I impulsively canceled on my friends, even though I was all dressed up, while they were waiting for me in a taxi in front of our building. It was unusual for me, but as I was walking down the stairs, instead of taking the elevator, I felt heavy in body and mind, which made me awful company.

When I told them I wasn't coming, I knew that they were disappointed, but they didn't make me feel any worse about it. After all, they had always known me as happy, loving Victoria who always had a smile on her face. I didn't want to go to the apartment and explain to my parents why I had stood up my closest friends, nor did I have the will to go anywhere else, so I just sat down, elegantly dressed, on the outside stairs, watching people exchanging taxis and Ubers or just walking with their heads bowed not noticing anything or anyone around them.

"We always have to be in a hurry of some kind." Walter politely sat next to me, always smiling, offering me a cushion to sit on since the steps were cold. "And the funniest thing of all, we are perfectly aware of it, but it doesn't bother us like it should. You were one of us, Victoria! So, what changed? I am just worried that something is going on, because it looks like you're not ok." Working the kind of job where he got to meet so many different people had made Walter pretty good at figuring out the troubles a person had just from their expressions.

"Sadly, you're right. You know me well, Walter, even though I'm not great with people. That's something I've come to realize. I'm not making excuses, but how I'm behaving is because of how helpless I feel. I'm torn between studying, finals, and helping people, one person in particular . . ."

Walter looked at me like a father looks at a lost child.

"Right now, this very second, what do you want the most? Say it out loud without thinking, and you'll know."

"To help Sean." Walter was right, as usual. In the pressure of the moment, my heart knew precisely where it belonged.

"See? It was a piece of cake. You had it in you the whole time; no need for drama or self-pity when the connection between the mind and heart is so clear. The hardest thing is to embrace what you want without thinking of anything else."

Walter's words made me smile. He had made me think about simple answers to what I thought were complicated questions. I had been overthinking again. It was tough to control my own mind. However, I also sensed that something was disturbing Walter's peace. I waited, to see if he would share it with me.

"Victoria, I usually never share this kind of secret while I'm working, and I don't usually share private details." The way he was talking reminded me of Grandpa A's serious conversations. "I am telling you this to help. We all have our obstacles in life. If my wife and I can manage to live a double life for our son's sake, you can find a solution to any problem. Nothing is impossible.

"*Double life* has a positive connotation in our lives. You see, our son Lance is a brilliant young man that got to go to Yale this year. How could I ever forget my wife's face when *that* envelope arrived. In our family, there has never been a college student, especially not at Yale University. We didn't even know he applied. And he didn't believe enough, even with his amazing records, he could get in. We grew up differently in the Bronx, not even thinking our kid might be one day the part of the prestigious Ivy League college. But also, as we are part of a small, distant family that wasn't ready to help at all, either because they were blinded with jealousy or because of old-fashioned views about education and work, the day came when we had to make a tough decision. It was our comfort or our son's education. My job brought a decent income, but my wife didn't have any at the time, and we didn't have enough money to fund both our comfort and his college tuition. We didn't own any realty, no large savings accounts, or huge retirement funds. So, at the beginning of his first semester, we had a decision to make. We sold only possession we have had; the old car Lance was born in one spring because we didn't make it to the hospital on time . . . Our little miracle . . ." Walter took a little break before continuing the story.

"The college costs turned out to be even bigger than *we* expected. Let's face it, my wife and I are simple people. We don't know anything about the colleges, and Lance was wrong not to believe in himself enough to apply for the financial aid along with the college submission. So, we have to cover this first year and we couldn't afford to rent even a small apartment we've lived in. But we have planned out that once every three to four months when Lance comes for holidays, we would rent the same apartment from an extremely good-hearted lady, God bless her, for almost nothing, so he won't feel guilty, and leave Yale. We just told him we decided to change the apartment because it was more convenient traffic-wise."

Something was way off in this story. I dared to interrupt Walter while he was still talking.

"Wait, Walter, where do you live for the other months of the year?"

I think it was the first time Walter had ever said those words to someone else.

"In a separate downtown shelters."

I felt numb.

When he saw my terrified look, he quickly added, "Nice people there. It is not how people think; homeless people aren't bad. They are just . . . lost. Aren't we all? Home or no home."

"I don't know what to say . . ." That was the most honest reaction I could muster; I was speechless, and now I felt ashamed of my own complaints while this beautiful man and his wife were suffering just to make their only son happy and accomplished. "I am so sorry, Walter. Is that okay to say?"

I realized that Walter was a living angel, never letting the joy go from his face, never feeling sorry for himself. Of course, he admitted he would like to have it more comfortable as he once had, but if it had to be like this, it was their current destiny.

"Don't worry, Victoria! It is life. We chose this path, the small white lie, living the way we live. It's only for a year. Lance might've had a chance for aid, but . . . We applied too late, they've already distributed all the grants for the year. And I have to admit, they were great about it—telling us we can do it next year. And we don't give up; it's not in our nature.

And then we just sat in silence. I wanted to ask Walter so much about family problems, crowdfunding, but he probably had an answer for it all. It didn't seem fair to torture him by responding to his confession with my curiosity.

But that same night, I had a clever thought; helping Walter and his wife could be the trigger for Sean's memories. After all, Grandpa A did say the way to retrieve Santa's memories was through good deeds.

The next morning, I woke up early, and searched the internet for the contacts I needed to call in the dean's office at Yale as well as the chairman's office. But no matter what I told them, no one let me past the front desk. All told, the front desk clerks refused to say anything because I couldn't tell them how, and if, I was related to the family.

I sat behind my desk, feeling numb, willing ideas to come to me.

*Nothing good ever comes from chasing answers without taking a break.*

And then a new idea came to me.

But *that* idea would require a lot of honesty, an apology, and a conversation with the one person I had been trying to avoid for the sake of the friendship: Tom.

Feeling scared of rejection, I got dressed and walked toward his home. It wasn't a short walk, but I needed air to clear my mind and choose the right words. The phrase "What goes around comes around" kept taunting me. It's funny how we never take our elders' advice seriously—instead, we end up hitting our heads later. Because of the scene a few weeks ago, I hadn't even announced my visit, so at least I was pretty sure he would open the door.

To say you're sorry, knowing it is totally your fault, is harder than telling a lie. Friendship wasn't supposed to involve being nasty or, in my case, insensitive.

Although I had known him my entire life, my hands were hopelessly shaky and my stomach in knots as I knocked on the massive door.

Tom opened the door himself, but there wasn't the slightest surprise on his face. He didn't even let me speak first. "I saw you from the window. I guess this needed to happen; better sooner than later."

I couldn't bear hearing him talk about us as if we were in a relationship and not as friends, but I had no right whatsoever to complain.

"Before I enter . . . I am truly sorry. That's the best I can do. For my behavior, words, and the fact I can't offer you anything but my hand in friendship. We both knew that from the start. With that being said, do you still want me to come in?" I gave him a choice, and could only hope he would make the one I needed.

"Of course. What are we, kids, to hold grudges?" Tom said, still firmly holding onto the handle, looking completely serious. At this moment, the man in front of me was no longer the child I had played in the sand with at five years old, but a serious adult whose pride and heart had been hurt.

"I need your help. Your dad was on a board of directors at Yale University, until five years ago?" There was no need to beat around the bush; he knew me better than that.

"Come inside. I know you love winter, but it is especially cold today."

We were still walking toward the living room, but I started telling him Walter's story. Tom was confused, surprised, and amazed, just as I was, and he didn't interrupt me. The fact was, we were longtime friends. You could tell it by the way Tom answered my yet unspoken question.

"To be honest with you, I am strictly prohibited from touching any of my father's information or work, but I can't shut my eyes in the face of their sacrifice. After all, it's only phone numbers you need, right?"

As he ordered me to wait and be on guard, Tom sneaked into his dad's office, logged into his business computer, and then wrote five numbers on a small piece of paper.

"Sorry, but my dad doesn't have any cell phone numbers on these files, just home ones along with addresses. In the past, he's had some serious issues with computer privacy."

I was grateful and didn't want to push it more, but it was too important for that.

"Oh, no. You have that look again. I can't."

"But . . . See my hypnotizing eyes . . . Pretty please."

"No, Victoria." Tom tried to stand by his words, he really did, but it was just a matter of time before he failed. "No. I can't give you the addresses. My father would kill me, caput, done. Finished."

After ten minutes of shameless imploring, Tom took me with him to the studio, opened the files, and then stepped out of the way. "Whatever you do, it is completely on you. I was never here, and my dad left his computer on by mistake."

"Thanks, Tom, you're a real friend."

"I know." He was trying hard to sound polite, but he couldn't hide his sorrowful tone every time he heard the word *friend*.

Only time would show him I wasn't *the one* for him and that he needed to open his heart to new adventures as well as different girls.

There was no time to lose. A lot of work was in front of me, while the proximity of the Christmas holidays made me worry that I was already too late.

Deep down, I was harboring the hope that helping Walter and his family would be indeed a special trigger to Sean's memory. If there was at least one percent of a chance of it working, I had to try it.

Not for Grandpa A, or the Winter Lands, but for the children of the future, so they could experience that special place too.

For two days in a row I tried to reach members of Yale's board, but I only got stupid excuses: "It's not up to us," "We need all five votes," "Paying the entire scholarship of one student would only create negative feelings in others and is not possible," and the list continued, putting responsibility on everybody else but themselves. I could finally understand what people went through when they had to go through business negotiations. It seemed these people could talk forever without saying anything intelligent or worth listening to.

Some people may think that I wasn't well enough prepared or didn't make a worthy enough effort, but eventually, the ticking clock pushed me into a corner. No wonder the craziest idea ended up coming to my mind.

During my research into the members of the board, I discovered some details from their lives which inspired the cards I decided to send them. All five of them did extraordinary things in life.

*A hand of kindness is better than a kind smile. A hand, the ones in need can take,*
*A smile they can only give back. BUT without the HAND would there be the SMILE?*
*IT IS ONLY MONEY,*
*BUT IT COULD MAKE THEM HAPPY.*

*Would You give up the comfort you enjoy for the benefit of your child?*
*IT IS ONLY MONEY*
*BUT IT COULD MAKE THEM HAPPY.*

*You're teaching your students and children to honor hard work and study, but at what cost? Would shelter break your wings?*
*IT IS ONLY MONEY*
*BUT IT COULD MAKE THEM HAPPY*

*Do you believe in giving the same kindness that once was gifted to YOU?*
*IT IS ONLY MONEY*
*BUT IT COULD MAKE THEM HAPPY*

*Having children is a blessing from above; the most beautiful thing in this world.*
*Would You gift a world to them?*
*IT IS ONLY MONEY*
*BUT IT COULD MAKE THEM HAPPY*

Each of the five members would receive a card with a unique short message, which was designed to trigger a particularly meaningful event in their lives. I planned on handing them out personally. Even though it wouldn't take long for the post office to deliver, I had this nervous feeling in me. I wanted this to succeed so badly, I had to make an effort to get in touch with these people personally.

It was important for me to present them with these cards before the weekly board meeting on the following Monday. That was in two days, which made it even harder to catch them, as no one likes to be interrupted during Saturday or Sunday relaxation.

"Where are you going now?" Joanna had been suspicious about my recent, unexplained excursions, though it was a worry mainly based in curiosity.

"I'm not trying to stick my nose where it doesn't belong."

*Oh no! As though she ever would.*

"But I have to deal with Mom's questions, monologues, and complaints about you, so give me a little credit."

And she was right. I knew how exhausting that was. Mom meant well, but she couldn't stop herself from talking; it was part of her.

"Listen, I can just say I'm working on a big project. If, and when, I complete it, I promise I'll tell you everything. But for now, the less you know, the better it will be because you won't have to lie to Mom."

Joanna angrily stepped in front of me. "Do you know how selfish you sound? You don't want to make anything about you, but all I hear is 'I this', 'I that'."

She took me by surprise and I didn't know what to reply.

"Oh well, consider it done." Joanna went from angry to calm in just a few seconds.

"But don't forget what you've promised."

Although the winter solstice was around the corner and the days were starting to get darker, it was surprisingly easy to deliver four of the letters to the board directors. However, for the fifth letter to the chairman of the board, I had to travel farther from home. Without telling anyone, I borrowed Dad's car, as he was on a business trip, and drove myself an hour and forty minutes from the city. I found the chairman's house, which was deep inside a vast property fenced with a high, thick hedge.

I had no choice but to push the intercom button on the outside of the house.

"Yes, please?" a pleasant voice asked two times before I answered. The connection was unsteady.

"Hello, can I personally deliver a letter to Chairman Ryan?"

"Family friend?"

"No. Look, I—"

"Is there any personal or business connection?"

"No."

"Then I'm afraid I can't put you through at this hour. You can schedule an appointment or leave the letter in the mailbox. Thank you."

"But it is really urgent."

"I do apologize. Goodnight."

Of course, people loved their security in this crazy world of ours, but this was too much. I was sure he was inside though, as I had seen him entering the house moments before I arrived; we had crossed paths at the light. Even though I never saw him until this night, it was easy to Google his picture.

I didn't hesitate for a long. I parked my car a block away so no one would notice it on a camera, and gave in to what would probably prove to be my dumbest decision ever. Who knew if I would be able to borrow Dad's car ever again after doing something like this?

What I did was wrong on so many levels. But we humans tend to do stupid things when we feel like we are trapped in a corner.

The fence was quite high, and the massive bushes weren't much help. But I somehow managed to climb, pushing foot after foot into the not-so-big holes in the fence, in order to overcome the only obstacle that lay between me and my goal.

What I didn't foresee was that as soon as I set my foot on the grass, other cameras caught me and the security alarm silently went off.

I was feeling ecstatic and full of adrenalin, in the expectation that I was going to make it to the fifth member before Monday. Of all the letters, I didn't want to push this one under the door. It had to be personally handed over to Chairman Ryan.

Even before I came onto the porch, the front doors opened abruptly, startling me.

"Who are you and what are you doing on my property at—" he nervously looked at the watch "—ten o'clock at night?" The man's posture in the barely opened doors and his voice seemed furious, and he had a big baseball bat in his hands. I could clearly see two older women hiding behind him, more in curiosity than fear.

I recognized him from his pictures on social media, in particular from his thick mustache.

"Chairman Ryan? I'm Victoria. I spoke to your secretary, a couple of times. As a matter of fact, with your security guard too! But . . ."

"You again? You don't know how to take *no* for an answer. It seems to me your hearing is bad. You will have a lot to explain soon, but to the police!"

In the heat of the moment, a few more words were exchanged between us, but my concentration shifted to one of the women, who was no longer hiding behind the chairman.

Now she was standing at the doors as well. It seemed like she was debating whether or not to take the letter from my hand. I could see there was at least a shadow of a doubt.

I decided I had no other choice than to play my last card.

"Didn't you give up your dream to save your grandchild?"

Maybe it was a bit too much, but Tom had called me that morning to let me know that Chairman Ryan has renounced his candidacy for the Senate so he could be close to his daughter and seven-year-old grandchild who was fighting a severe auto-immune illness. I know, it wasn't my right to say it, but he did take one step back, possibly confused by how I got that information. His wife was looking at him now.

Anything could have happened at that point, but the dean was saved by blue and red lights rapidly approaching his driveway.

"I think it is time to say goodnight." He pushed his wife inside, but not before she grabbed the letter from my hand and closed the doors, turning her back on me.

Then it was between four police officers and me. And it didn't go well.

Nevertheless, all in all, everything I had done was for a good cause. Chairman Ryan had the letter with the card at his house, and the police escorted me along with Dad's car to the nearest precinct. No matter how bad my decisions were, I felt a sense of peace knowing I really had done my best to help Walter. Although getting arrested hadn't been part of my plan.

It wasn't like I imagined it to be, nothing like it looks in TV shows. They don't put you into the jail right away like some hardcore criminal. Police officers listened calmly to what I had to say, which wasn't a lot, as I obviously couldn't tell them anything about the Winter Lands. As a result, I failed to justify my actions. They did, however, kindly offer me the right to a phone call.

"You better call your parents."

Oh, I knew better than that.

Instead, my choice of call was risky and unwise. I didn't want to scare my parents again.

But there was one person whose number I hadn't dialed in a while, and he did kind of want to see me as soon as possible. I decided that this was the right moment.

Brian. I knew I could trust him. I always had. When he came to the police station to bail me out, after almost two and a half hours due to heavy traffic, I was really embarrassed even though I had been the one who called him. I just couldn't find the words. Brian and I filled out the paperwork in awkward silence. The police officer behind the desk probably thought we were a married couple in the middle of a fight. Brian didn't seem to know what to say either. I guess the police precinct was the last place on earth he would expect to find me.

After ten minutes, while I was walking toward the car, he finally started to talk. "Victoria, I came here with a friend, Jack." He pointed to someone leaning against his car. "Since you told me the police had your car too, your dad's car, I thought I'd drive you back home myself, and Jack will take my car back."

The guy who was a bit chubby, with a kind face, was cracking up with laughter. "Well, isn't this the most dangerous criminal in the States? Please don't break into my house. I have one Rottweiler and two Beagles, and I'm not guaranteeing your safety."

That joke didn't make much sense, but his facial expressions were too funny not to laugh back, so I gave him the satisfaction of a laugh.

Amid all the laughter, I still felt troubled by Brian's silent treatment as I got into my car, and we pulled away from the precinct.

"Okay, I just think you should say what's on your mind." I couldn't take it anymore.

"Did you really think that breaking and entering was the only solution to whatever you had to resolve? All alone. Fifty miles away from home, in the middle of the night, sneaking onto the grounds of someone in a position of authority like that?" Brian was worried sick, as well as furious.

When he said it that way, I could see my plan hadn't been a plan at all, just a dumb improvisation pushed by time and events.

"Not quite sure what to tell you . . ."

"When we agreed to start over again, we made a pact—to be there for each other. You didn't even think I could help you?"

I felt the urge to cry. Never before had I felt so ashamed.

"I bet you didn't think. And taking your dad's car? What did you—?"

"No! I didn't think!" I interrupted him, already humiliated enough. Suddenly all my emotions were transformed into tears, which had been happening a lot lately.

I wanted too much from life at once. And at the same time, something in me didn't understand that there were easier roads I could have chosen. I have always leaned toward goofy rushed solutions and the most difficult paths.

Brian stopped the car in the emergency lane.

"I am so sorry that I yelled at you like that, but you need someone close to point out another angle of your actions. Don't cry, Vicky . . . Don't cry." He gently wiped the tears from my red cheeks. He had always been a gentleman, I remembered that as he came close and pressed a kiss full of love onto my forehead. I was in his protective arms, sitting quietly, trying to calm myself down.

"Victoria, you have to know I will always be here for you. I will be the voice of reason you sometimes lack. I think it's time to go!"

While he was driving, Brian took my hand in his, like it was only natural.

It calmed me down.

Once we were in front of my building, Brian stopped the car in front of Walter, who was beside himself because he had been the one who saw me leaving with the car in the first place, before my adventure took a wrong turn.

"Young lady, what did you do? Do your parents know you took the car? You didn't even gave me chance to ask you anything before you left. Who is this boy?" He just couldn't stop being a father figure to everyone.

"You are still calling me 'young lady'?" I had kind of missed seeing his face today. "I just had to run an errand that wasn't able to be postponed."

Oh my! I wanted to tell him so badly what I had tried to do for him this evening, even if it was a failure. He had to know that someone was doing their best to make the world a better place.

Without any additional explanation, I went upstairs and fell on the bed tired and still dressed.

Sleep overcame me as soon as my head touched the pillow.

The next morning, waking up was anything but sweet.

"Victoria! Get up this instant! Everybody is waiting for you in the living room."

My mom burst into my room without knocking on the door. That wasn't unusual, but her tone was colder than Canada in midwinter. I didn't know what was going on since everything still felt like a dream, but I knew I'd figure it out soon enough.

A deep breath to calm my nerves was in order before I stepped into the living room. I thought they had probably figured out I took the car the day before.

But there was a big surprise waiting for me.

In the middle of the living room, my parents were sitting comfortably together with Chairman Ryan. Then came a monologue like the one you would hear in a movie, the likes of which I had heard many times coming from my mom, only in different circumstances: "Imagine our beautiful surprise," she started ironically, "having a stranger at our door, no less than a Chairman of Yale University, early in the morning, telling us he would not press charges against our daughter for trespassing! Politely, I tried to explain it to him it wasn't our daughter he was talking about, but . . ." Mom took a dramatic break in the monologue, giving herself a chance to take a breath, "it all fell apart when he showed me the security footage of my sweet, always well-behaved daughter parking her dad's car, which she took without asking anyone, in a neighboring driveway and climbing over a fence onto another man's property."

Of course, why hadn't it crossed my mind that entire luxurious neighborhood like that would have cameras everywhere?

I didn't say a word for a moment or two. The truth had been spoken. The only thing that came into my head was that I felt grateful to Chairman Ryan . "Thank you for not pressing any charges. I didn't mean any harm."

Mom was out of her mind with fury and couldn't even look at me, and to make things worse my dad was here too; he came early morning from the business trip.

Joanna was eavesdropping from the hallway, and I actually think she finally, in some weird way, was proud of me for doing something crazy and out of the ordinary. For her, I had just lost my title of 'Miss Does Everything Perfect' so she could relax and enjoy the fact we were equally imperfect.

Chairman Ryan stood up. "Then you have to give thanks to my wife. She reminded me of who I was before and what I did for my family when my grandchild got sick. Even though I usually don't do any favors because it wouldn't be fair toward other students, I had an early board meeting where we agreed to give out the financial aid to Lance for this year also, reversing our initial decision, which was prompted by his late request."

I was in disbelief, and trying hard not to burst into tears—yet again.

"But there are conditions, of course." Chairman Ryan tried to sound harsh, but there was excitement somewhere in his deep voice that he couldn't hide. "Lance must maintain high grades above a certain level to our expectations, and we do expect a lot. He will be checked on regularly, and there will be no room for mistakes."

Joanna, Mom, and Dad didn't understand what we were talking about, but they calmed down after hearing that spark of pride in the dean's tone.

Lately, people had been leaving me speechless way too often.

"I'm sure Lance will do his best." The next breath I took was the lightest I had taken since I had come home from the Winter Lands.

Chairman Ryan tried hard to maintain his strict persona. "And, Victoria, please stay away from other people's houses if not invited. I'd suggest a criminal career is not the best choice for you since you got caught on your first attempt. Now, if you'd excuse me, I have serious matters to attend."

I had been hoping he wouldn't remind my parents of what I did, but I guess being a parent himself, he wanted me to face the consequences of my actions. And it didn't really feel like a lecture, just a reminder of what I had done.

"Chairman Ryan?"

"Yes?" He was already at the door, but he turned back to hear what I had to say.

"Could I ask you one more favor?"

He couldn't believe my nerve. "You really think—"

"Don't tell Lance why he got the financial aid now. I don't want him to know or feel guilty about what his parents went through. Let them decide to tell him the whole story, if and when they want. Please."

Chairman Ryan looked at me, astonished. Maybe he thought I would have wanted to take all the credit for what had happened.

"And I suppose you have already an idea of what should we do exactly?" I could hear the irony in his tone.

But he didn't intimidate me. " They should call Walter to tell him good news! His shift is over tomorrow after five o'clock in the afternoon, and he will be able to take the phone call."

Chairman Ryan was quiet for awhile.

"I will see if that is possible." He didn't want to reveal more than he already did.

He also told me I had to pay off my intrusion from the other night somehow. So, he ordered me to help with the new foundation Yale University was preparing, as my community service work. It would help poor but excellent students, not only by giving them scholarships but also by giving them a hand with accommodations, food, and everything else required for college life, including educating them about the application itself.

My redemption would be everything but bitter, he said.

After the chairman left, Mother Dearest just couldn't control the strength of her voice for the next thirty minutes, while my dad cut in, every so often to highlight her words of how stupid what I did was.

"Still selfish." Johanna passed right by me, making sure I didn't have her approval either.

Obviously, I didn't say anything to argue, and apologies were on repeat throughout the day, but they were also surprised when they heard the real story about who I had decided to help and why. No one could be indifferent when they heard Walter's story.

The entire day I stayed home anxiously waiting for tomorrow to come. I was planning to be by Walter's side when he'd receive the call.

The next day, in the evening, amid new snowflakes, I rushed as fast as I could to meet Walter before the end of his shift.

"Walter, Walter, Walter!" I kept nervously calling him like an idiot until a new boy at the reception desk directed me to search outside.

"Where's the fire, Vicky?" he'd clearly heard me screaming.

I took a deep breath, filling my lungs with air like I was the wolf ready to blow down the three little pigs' homes, only with good news.

"Merry Christmas, Walter!" I hugged him firmly like I would never let go.

"B—But Victoria, what on earth is going on with you? It is still a while until Christmas." Walter seemed embarrassed by my emotional outburst. His shift hadn't finished, and I was shamelessly yelling at him in front of clients, and strangers, in the middle of the street.

I his hand in mine.

"When your phone rings—answer it right away!"

We didn't have to wait long. At precisely five o'clock, Walter's cellphone rang.

He tried his best to answer it with the big klutzy gloves that kept his hands warm, but he needed a little help.

"Victoria, who is it?" Walter was confused, trying to hand me the phone.

"Don't ask me, ask them."

Time seemed to come to a standstill as he looked at me without a word.

Was it disbelief? Happiness? Sadness? Gratitude?

Probably all those. It was priceless.

"But, Victoria . . ." His voice was shaky. ". . . they said . . . Lance has got full financial aid until he graduates if his grades stay as they are, starting with this semester already. Is this a joke? How? Who? Why they've called me now after telling us we were too late? I don't understand."

No matter how good his heart was, you could see doubt in those two lovely old eyes. "Something like this doesn't just happen for no reason."

"It is all true, Walter. They heard everything about you and your wife's situation and finally decided to help out."

"But . . ."

I just smiled. "No buts, Walter. This is your reality now."

Now I had to break the promise I had made to myself not to tell him anything since he couldn't accept this call as real. He really had a hard time believing it, so I sat him down on the stairs, as had been our habit lately, and quietly revealed what had happened since he told me his unbelievable life story.

Then he finally believed what I was saying, as he could connect the events from the past few days, and he knew I was crazy enough in a good way to do everything I told him.

At that point, he started to cry, and he couldn't stop. The weight life had put on his shoulders had finally been relieved. I still had one gift to give him. It was a Christmas ornament in the shape of a present—nothing extraordinary looking, but very special in meaning because I had got it from the Winter Lands' Christmas tree under the Crystal Mountains.

"Can I gift you this?" He could barely look at me through his tears, but he was listening nevertheless. "This has exceptional value to me, and I want to give it to you, in this special moment of your life."

He took it from my hands, speechless, and put it in his pocket.

"And don't worry about Lance. Chairman of the board and I have a special agreement that they won't discover the true story behind all of this until you and your wife decide to tell him."

"Victoria . . ." he found the strength to start, but I cut him off.

"I know. Just call your lady and share the great news about Lance!"

He quickly stood up, and gave me a kiss on the forehead. "I'll never forget."

And then a thought crossed my mind: Sean was probably lonely and waiting for me. I started to run with my mind already on that bench.

*Why I never asked him if he owns a cellphone now?*

He was sitting there, as always.

When he saw me, his eyes brightened, and his smile grew wider.

"I am so sorry! I swear I didn't forget you, but—"

Sean interrupted me by raising his hand into the air, like an order. "Are you by any chance the girl that harassed the entire board of directors of Yale just to help one student in need? An hour ago, I overheard a strange conversation in which an older lady was complaining about the manners of a girl who trespassed into their house just to ask for a favor . . . She was outraged. Somehow, I knew that must be you. But I need to hear it from you. Tell me it was you, Victoria."

"I am not proud of that but—yes."

I could see the fireworks in his eyes as he jumped off the bench and started dancing with joy. It reminded me of a moment when Grandpa A had done the same back in the Winter Lands. The happiness and excitement took over every passerby, infected by his laughter.

"I knew it, I knew it, I knew it was you!" He was completely out of it because joy had just knocked on his soul's doors after a long time away.

"You're one of a kind. A person that never gives up. Oh, when I think of what you did, it makes me think of the time Toby—just to fix our chocolate machine—worked day and night. He wouldn't listen to anyone telling him it was impossible. He just went against everyone, even Avery and I, to prove us wrong . . ." He continued talking, to my awe, but I didn't dare stop him. Unaware of it, he was remembering the Winter Lands. My good deed did exactly I was praying for—he was unlocking lost memories. "We said it was an ancient machine and that its time had come to an end. We were in a panic, trying to figure out how to create a new machine, but he wasn't ready to give up, thanks to a gut feeling he had about the old machine. And he proved us wrong, all because he had such a strong belief in himself and the machine. And, look, it is still working wonders. The whole Winter Lands was proud of him. If you believe in something strongly enough, prove it. Forget what others think and work on yourself and the goal."

It was hard to believe my ears, but Sean was actually talking about the Winter Lands as though he had never left.

"You remember!"

Sometimes, all we need is a small push to remember our values and memories.

All Sean Christmas's heart wanted from this world was a human gesture that would ease the bad things he witnessed after leaving his home.

He was looking at me as though he was going over each word he had just said to me in his head, only to finally understand.

"Victoria, I think I might know where my home is."

We both smiled. Sean still didn't remember who he was, and no matter how crazy and magical the details about his hometown from his memories might seem, an immense weight was lifting, leaving him open to dream while awake.

*Dear Santa,*

*(Dear Cadelia, Rudolf and Grandpa A)*

*I feel terrible for my complete silence, but I have been busy with the task you entrusted me with. Proudly, and with a strong belief in myself, but still a bit scared, I did find Sean Christmas almost three weeks ago but couldn't find the courage in me to share this vital information with you and the Winter Lands. But somewhere along the path, even though Sean still wasn't remembering anything, I found everything I was looking for in others. Mr. Christmas still doesn't recall his past life, but he does have fragments of memories involving the Winter Lands, you, Grandpa A, and Toby. It is kind of funny, but thinking about talking animals made him have the same reactions as I had when I met Rudolf.*

*Ah, good old Rudolf! Sean is a little scared of the big bear he keeps meeting in his dreams, but hopefully this will change soon enough. I hope you will forgive my insensitivity for not writing back.*

*Sending my love to you, Cadelia, and all of you with a promise that I'll bring Santa Claus back where he truly belongs!*

*Love,*

*Victoria!*

*PS: He is starting to have white hair in spots again. That can only be a good sign, right?*

# Vintage Heart of the City

"Where are you going now?" Mom stood in front of the doors. "Victoria, don't forget what you did with Chairman Ryan. But still you are disappearing without explanation." She looked at me, more worried than angry. I understood why, but how could I tell her anything without revealing things they just couldn't know? "Now, I get you're twenty-six, but this is no way to act. Not while you're living under my roof."

And there it was, the most famous sentence mothers use all around the world. It was totally fair, too, but if I told her what had happened to me, would she believe it? No. I loved my mother so much, but some things had to stay only with me.

"Mom, can I say something in my defense? Have you forgotten I told you yesterday about getting together with Chairman Ryan to discuss the fundraising event?" This was true, but not entirely so, and Mom guessed I was holding something back. "Listen, Mom," I started to apologize, "before that, I'll be going to Central Park for a walk to visit an old friend working there. He is a really nice elderly man who likes to talk with me, which helps him not feel alone."

Mom liked this version of the truth better since she knew that sounded more like me: it wouldn't have been the first time I found a lost soul and spent my free time talking with them.

I gave her a kiss on the forehead.

"Mom, I'm sorry if I disappointed Dad and you, but in that specific millisecond I didn't see any other choice, and I felt I had to give my best. Helping Walter was a promise I made to myself. If I'd failed, to him, it wouldn't change anything since he wasn't aware of my intentions and plans, but I would have known. Maybe I could've done things differently, but I am who I am, learning by my own mistakes and admitting responsibility, just as *you* taught me. Isn't that part of life too? Not everything can be pink sparkles."

I gave her a big kiss on the cheek and went out before she managed to process what had been said. Maybe she was even starting to see me as an adult.

When I ran outside, Walter was nowhere to be found. The concierge told me he'd taken the day off. My heart skipped as I daydreamed about a family day spent together, maybe they were even planning on renting a new apartment. Just thinking about it made me happy.

Today, the scenery around the bench was the same, but the person on it was clearly changed. As I approached, I could see those warm red cheeks smiling as Sean waved at me. He looked like a man reborn, and he was surrounded by parents and their children while telling them stories.

The children, with their natural innocence, clearly recognized the great good in him. But Sean's psychological change wasn't the only thing that had changed. In a short time, he had developed occasional gray streaks in his hair, his beard was growing a little faster, and the red color didn't seem to be planning on leaving his cheeks anytime soon.

I believed that somewhere deep inside, he half knew his identity but was too scared to allow himself to accept it as reality. The moment he spotted me, Sean apologized to the kids and ran to meet me halfway.

"Victoria!" He sounded overexcited but spoke cautiously, so no one else could hear him. "I still can't remember anything new, but the cold now feels familiar and warm. My mind can clearly see interwound mountain chains so high you can't see where they end, with breathtaking, sharp, mirror-like lakes and endless forests. It is so magical, but I feel in my bones that the place is real. Awake or asleep, I see the scenery constantly calling my name. And, oh, how wonderful those dreams are!"

Sean just couldn't stop talking, describing to me familiar details of the Winter Lands. How could I keep that happiness contained?

"It is real. You're not crazy, and those are definitely not vague dreams, but an amazing place called the Winter Lands. It is your hometown, and it is finding its way back into your memories at a slow but sure pace."

Sean gave me a relieved look. "Which of them is a real memory?"

"All of them! Everything you see in your mind is as real as you and I talking here and now. Those places are separate here, because of our mind's limits, but in reality, they are connected through snow, and all a part of the place called the Winter Lands. Each location is an extraordinary place where magical things happen. And I had the great honor to visit the land not so long ago. As your memories come back, you will remember too. I don't have a doubt about it, not anymore."

Sean was a bit perplexed but didn't argue, which pushed me into continuing. "Now, I don't know if it's going to work, but to speed up the memories, I have an idea. We are going to walk all of New York in search of a good deed."

Sean gave me a look. "Walk? Don't forget, young lady, I'm not that youthful anymore."

"Don't worry, Sean, today will be just a preview of something much bigger. I'm still not sure exactly what, but I'm getting there. I have just the right thing for now."

I loved the carriage rides, but only from people I knew were taking good care of their horses, so I stopped one near us.

"Mister! Excuse me! Mister!" I ran toward a coachman. "Is your horse well rested and fed?" He looked offended so I rephrased the question: "Not to offend you, but I would need to pay for a five-hour ride. I don't want the poor animal to get tired."

The coachman looked at me like I didn't know what I just asked of him.

"I'll be honest with you: five hours will cost you a lot, and may I remind you we don't have permission to enter the traffic. It would be risky for you and my beautiful horses. You know? So, what's circling going to do to you and my horses in those awfully long five hours?"

"Okay, that's fair. You know the regulations better than I do. Then two hours it is, and take us everywhere you can go, of course, keeping in mind we will have to improvise a few stops along the way. I will pay extra for your effort."

He smiled cheerfully. "Done."

"Mr. Christmas, come on. It's time to go."

The coachman turned toward us, laughing again. "It's like having Santa Claus in my carriage." He continued to laugh, but little did he know it was the absolute truth.

"Where are we off to?"

"Nowhere and everywhere. You'll see."

Before going out, I put some of my savings in my backpack, along with ornaments and tiny toys just to show Sean that there is kindness in every human. It was a tradition I did every year before Christmas; only, this time, Santa needed to see it, feel the joy. I hoped it would trigger more of his memories.

"Victoria, why is everything such a mystery with you?" He was suspicious but didn't stop me.

I was planning on taking him to see people doing small but kind things for each other, like a young person carrying groceries for an elderly lady, kids sharing toys, people engaging with strangers to say something beautiful just because they felt someone needed a friendly word.

Our first stop was next to some homeless people. We helped each with some money and a warm meal we had bought on our way. Each grateful look that was given to us, each smile made Sean more at ease as he saw how we were helping them. However, that wasn't what had the strongest effect on him. It was actually seeing other people doing the same thing, offering help with no hesitation, whether it was with food, money, or a handshake, it didn't matter.

Who were we to judge someone's life and tell if he or she was worth it or not? Why is it so hard to help each other without over-thinking? Oh, how many times had I heard: but they will buy alcohol or something else that is bad, we shouldn't reward their laziness, and so on.

Who were we to judge?

I openly admit to being like that once, until I realized my life was blessed with everything: family, friends, health, and love, so why would I be afraid to share that happiness? It's not like it was going to be stolen from me. Until today I couldn't give the exact answer to these questions. But it was great to see how many other people had had a change of heart too.

One special moment brought tears to Sean's eyes—a little six-year-old girl approached a nineteen-year-old adolescent to give her her own red shawl, not noticing how small it was for her. The little one didn't say a word, but with her mother's blessing she took her scarf off and placed it around the older girl's neck with her tiny hands.

"Always protect your neck. My mommy keeps telling me this, but now she'll have to close her eyes." The child took her mother's hand and continued to walk. Even at that age, she knew not to wait for a thank you.

The adolescent girl started sobbing when Sean Christmas touched her shoulder. "This too will pass. Just find the courage in you to change things. No matter what money, clothing, or help you receive, if you don't change, the change won't follow you. You were always a good girl, Clara."

And that was what it took. Later, Sean told me that he couldn't know if his words had made it through the girl's anxious thoughts about her harsh life, but that it was a moment he would cherish forever. Saying those words, and knowing her name from *The Naughty or Nice List* made him remember everything. Now he knew who he had been, was, and would be again.

He burst with excitement, taking my hands and spinning both of us in circles until we collapsed into the piles of snow.

"Victoria, I don't know if I'm dreaming while awake, but I can feel my whole life again!" Then he whispered sweet words for my ears only: "I can sense who's happy or sad, scared or fearless," and then added, chuckling, "naughty or nice!" It was really cute the way he covered his mouth as he said that. "I can't believe I actually said that!"

It was clear that the kindness of the people we had met had opened Sean's mind to the world of the Winter Lands and allowed him to overcome any remaining doubt.

I had the real Santa Claus in front of me. Once lost, now found.

It had taken twenty years to bring him to his senses, but the best of it was that it was humans, with all their flaws, who had finally undone the wrong, and allowed the Winter Lands to shine with more light.

*Dear Santa,*
*(Dear Cadelia, Rudolf and Grandpa A)*

*He remembers everything!*
*Please let me know what's the best way to bring him back*
*to you.*
*Thank you,*
*Victoria!*

*PS: Hi, Rudie!*

When I came home afterward, still delighted and beside myself, there was another gathering of King Arthur's round table—I saw my mom's, dad's, and sister's worried faces.

"What's going on?" Of course, I knew what was on the menu, my behavior, but that didn't stop me from asking.

"Victoria, sit, please."

Dad started this time. "Your psychology professor called today to check on you, wondering if everything is okay since you skipped a couple of classes. Being one of your favorite classes, it got her worried. And to our surprise, it has happened twice in only a month."

There was an uncomfortable silence. My parents probably just wanted to hear a simple explanation of why this was happening. Perhaps they even expected a small lie that would help them feel better, but it wasn't my way. At least not any more.

"You got me. I don't have anything to say, to be honest. Days I allow myself to skip college might seem odd to you since I never allow myself to skip classes. And you knew me, until now—of course, as the good, obedient daughter. That is mainly my fault for not letting you see who I really am, since I've always been so scared of being judged by you two—two perfectionist. But everything was well calculated on my behalf. None of my skipped classes will mess with my points or exams. After helping Walter, I had another project of my own, where I needed to find a real home for a lost old man. And today, I think I did. There is no way I can feel sorry, embarrassed, or guilty, and I can't apologize knowing I'm doing the right thing. What I am sorry for, is not actually being able to tell you more."

They just stared at me, so I continued talking, a skill I had learned from my mom.

"Look, don't take my words for rudeness. I would understand your worry if I did something horrible like use drugs or alcohol, which I never would, but this is about helping people, and even so, I only took time off from classes to gift my time to others in need. It could affect my future only by bringing me the same happiness I put on their faces. So, no family intervention, please. Maybe you still can't see the change in me is positive, but I am still the same old Victoria who knows her principles—which I've stretched a bit, and only for that I am sorry."

It came out too harshly, so I tried to remedy my words. "When I finish with my projects of helping people, I promise to show you everything. It is hard, but most of it I have filmed on my cellphone or camera. And every single time I'm out there doing good, you're there, a big part of me. Now, excuse me I have a lot of work to do."

After that, I went back to my room, giving them time to think about what I said. I felt dizzy with laughter but then my eyes saw the Winter Land's envelope, this time on the chair.

*Dear Victoria,*

*Our faith in you has paid off. A strong-willed heart can do unimaginable things, which you proved once more by bringing back Sean's memories.*
    *Santa Claus is back.*
    *With that, I have to tell you that, as soon as your letter*

*came, the toy manufacturer granted us an opportunity to change the verdict to our benefit by scheduling an appointment with us to see if he will continue our life-long collaboration. This will require you to come here with Santa to the Winter Lands as soon as possible. If someone can resolve this, it would be you together with Sean. Don't worry about not being home. You will be away for just three full days, so make sure you set everything up with your family and friends. We will, in the future, try to make exceptions when it comes to our strict rules, so you get to share it all with your family. For now, it has to be like this.*

*Tomorrow at 0030, be in Central Park at the location attached to this letter with Sean Christmas.*

*Lots of kisses,*
*Grandpa A, Cadelia, and Rudolf*
*by Rudie: Hi, Vicky!*

"Wow."

Maybe to Grandpa A, from the Winter Lands' point of view, that seemed really easy, but he had never met my parents.

I immediately set to work, but this time I had to rely on the loyalty of my sister.

I called Joanna into my room and explained what I needed from her, and then waited expectantly for her reply.

"First, where are you going? What stunt are you pulling now? Second, and far more important, what do I get for lying to our parents?" Joanna looked at me suspiciously. Some things between us always remained the same. We were sisters, what else could I expect?

"Please, for once be the sister who doesn't ask but trusts. If you do me this favor, one day I'll take you where I'm going. I have to go or there won't be any toys for the kids."

My words probably didn't make any sense to her, but it was worth trying.

"Have I got this right? You want me to lie to Mom and Dad, which is totally not cool, that you went to Lisa's over the weekend to study. I also have to send text messages from your phone and sometimes even leave them pre-recorded voice messages all while you're going to an unknown place, without me being able to contact you, so you can save . . . toys and maybe one day even take me somewhere I don't know about?" She looked at me like I was out of my mind. But then she gave me an unexpected answer: "Okay. Sounds fun." But she quickly added, "Oh, I will get to enjoy the moment when they figure out you lied again!"

My sister. How could I not love her? A tough character, but when I really needed her, even if she pretended otherwise, she was always going to be there for me.

I called Lisa, asking her for a huge favor too, but first apologizing for my behavior and explaining everything to her saying more or less the same thing I had told Joanna. She also made it her mission to find out what I was planning but eventually agreed.

When I had every detail set, I started to jump up and down on the bed.

That was my thing: to think of a happy memory I have had, and then start jumping, dancing, or singing.

# Back to the Winter Lands
## with a New Truth

On Friday morning, at 0030 sharp, Sean and I were standing at the rendezvous point in Central Park, still debating how they were planning on picking us up in the middle of the busiest city in the world without being noticed by anyone. Sean was trying to remember how it usually happened, but he knew it wasn't the reindeer since they mostly used them close to the ground because, in his words, it was much easier to go under the radar. All at once, we heard the sound of an aircraft engine coming from the side where the meadow met the park trees. But we didn't see anything coming from that direction.

"Oh, no!" I said, as I remembered the last time. "I hope they didn't send that lunatic who apparently finds big storms a personal challenge. It's like some kind of contest for him."

Automatically I started to run toward the sound, leaving Sean Christmas behind me, with nothing left to do but start running after me. Even though I couldn't see anything in front of me, I suddenly collided with the place. I was wondering why I hadn't seen it until now. Thankfully, this part of Central Park was always a little deserted during the nighttime, so there wasn't a risk of anybody else stumbling upon the invisible wall.

Shortly after that, I saw Mr. Larry's grumpy face that slowly took on a shy smile—it was a bit creepy, but a smile nevertheless—once he saw Sean behind me. I knew it wasn't anything to do with me.

"So, Miss isn't-it-better-to -stay-out-of-the-snowstorm did it after all? You found the man himself. Congrats." I had a worried expression on my face, wondering how he had managed to land a plane in the middle of Central Park's Sheep Meadow without anyone noticing. Although, thinking about it, I hadn't spotted the plane either, though my knee was sore from the collision, which only made me more curious.

"Is Miss worried about something?" Larry couldn't miss the chance to rub it in my face again, and my confused look was clearly pure entertainment to him.

"No. I'm just thinking how interesting the front page of tomorrow's newspapers will be if we don't move along."

"Once a party pooper, always a party pooper. Don't worry, Miss. No one will ever notice us. They are too busy in their everyday lives to notice the magical things happening in front of them. Faith and belief are what this world needs, Victoria. Even though you're learning it now, you're still far from being a master."

That was actually true, so I didn't feel the urge to respond.

Finally, Sean Christmas caught up. He was breathless, managing to take in air only through his mouth.

"Victoria, child, you can't simply run away from me like a maniac. Oh, hello, Larry. Finally getting older, but no less cranky, are ya?" Sean was mimicking the pilot's talk. "Nice to see you again, old friend!"

For the first time, Larry took off his sunglasses, and I swear I could see one glistening tear in the corner of his eye as Santa recognized him.

Santa couldn't understand why we were both giving him strange looks, but we were totally okay with it—in fact it was the first time the pilot and I had ever agreed on anything.

From that moment on, Larry didn't stop whistling happy songs. He was like a changed man.

Once we were inside the plane, my mind went back in time, two months to be exact. The plane, as always, had a Christmassy mood, but there was a different book waiting for me on the table. *Peter Pan.* How appropriate!

I took a wild guess that Rudolf had had something to do with the book choice, remembering the child in me who refused to fully grow up. So his choice made sense.

Sean was excited to get on the plane again.

He knew exactly which cabinet to find coffee in and about the secret compartment where the pilot hid his salty donuts. It was fun watching him just being himself.

However, now we found ourselves just waiting on the ground.

"Mr. Larry, why aren't we in the air? I am kind of short on time since, you know," I said like it was a tiny detail, "my family can't know about my whereabouts."

As usual he had a sarcastic retort ready. "We are waiting for one more person to join us." He didn't give much information, but he couldn't contain himself. "Did you seriously think you were the first one sent here to find Sean Christmas? There is this boy, now a man, who found Sean Christmas several years ago, but he couldn't get through to him. . . Sean's head wasn't in the right place."

Then he started to murmur to himself, and I couldn't understand a word he said. And he continued to talk to himself, a bit louder this time. "I could never make myself say 'Santa.' For goodness sake, we're the same age! I believe, but to call him *that.* No, no, and *no.*

That's *Sean* for me."

Five minutes later, someone outside knocked on the door making Larry get up from his seat. "Late again, aren't ya? All you pretty boys think everything is okay."

Then a voice I knew so well replied, "Sorry, Larry! Business as usual. Not all of us get to drive a plane as a job."

It was Brian's voice; I was sure of it before I even saw his face.

When he lowered his head, making an entrance, my eyes confirmed the scarcely believable message my ears had sent me. With his signature compelling smile, he was looking at me directly, not letting my look go, not for a second. I was utterly overcome by all sorts of emotions. The words escaped me, so I just sat unable to hide the shock.

Brian knew me well, so he didn't say a word as he stopped to greet Sean. While he talked to Santa, in my head I was replaying every moment since Brian had re-entered my life as the secret Flash on Columbus Day. I saw now that all of it had been part of the Winter Lands' plan to finally involve me in a search. And when the heat hit my cheekbones, I had to admit to myself I was feeling baffled about what I felt for Brian now.

What was true? Were the kisses staged too, like the dance, the airport collision between us, him always showing up when I needed encouragement to continue with my mission?

How complicated is the human brain? I thought to myself.

Why wasn't I wondering how long Brian had known about Sean? Whether or not he had been to the Winter Lands before? And how long he had worked for them? Instead, my heart was focusing only on how honestly he had behaved toward me.

I couldn't say hello yet, so I continued to listen to him and Sean, talking together after Larry finally took us up airborne.

Sean finally turned toward me. "Victoria, meet Brian, my favorite young man. You see, now I can connect all the little dots. I met

Brian six years ago. He was the son of my business partner, bright young guy, eager to learn all about financial advising. Now I understand he knew about me since the first minute; he was the one pushing his dad to introduce us. Somewhere along the road, he started to help me regain my memories. But unfortunately, we didn't have a breakthrough, and that pushed me into more significant despair as I had left the job for the one in Central Park.

Nevertheless, he promised to take care of my well-being, have daily conversations with me, and that's what kept me sane. But lately, since he became a big shot in the investment world, he was traveling more, so we haven't see each other for a few months now. Such a bright man." Clearly, Sean was also mesmerized by Brian.

He was surprised to see there wasn't any communication between Brian and me, but he decided to leave it aside.

Throughout the flight, it was a game of looks between us—some that made me want to go to Brian and kiss and hug him, and others that made me want to slap his face for concealing the truth. But who was I to complain? I had done the same thing to my parents.

They spent a while catching up on the news while I pretended to read a book and listen to music with my earphones on.

But I couldn't concentrate. I could feel Brian's occasional glance, as he was presumably trying to figure out the right time to talk and give his explanation.

I heard everything that was said among them, and I appreciated Sean for not trying to involve me in the conversation.

"So, did you finally meet the right girl?"

Brian caught my look with an invisible lasso, as though he knew I was listening, and didn't have the intention of letting it go. "I did. She's everything I could hope for. And more. Crazy enough to take my breath away, a beautiful soul, and when she looks at me, the whole world disappears in her eyes, making me want her even more with each passing day. When she's not around me, I lean on the movie in my head of every meeting we had in the past just so I can smell her perfume, gaze into her eyes, and revive the kisses we shared. That's called love."

I blushed instantly, lowering my look, and pretending there was something interesting in the book I had read at least fifty times.

My thoughts eventually calmed down so I could sleep. My brain had been working overtime lately, and though excitement was making me feel light and amazed, it was also draining my body, telling me it was time to rest for a minute or two. Tired beyond words and already starting to dream, I smelled Brian's cologne next to me, and felt someone taking away *Peter Pan* and covering me gently with a blanket.

"Wake up, Victoria. I'm home!" Sean happily shook my shoulders.

He didn't wait for pilot Larry to open the door. He did it himself. He couldn't wait to step outside and smell the familiar scent of nature, of his home he'd lost for almost twenty years. Sean was visibly moved.

"I am incredibly grateful to the residents of the Winter Lands for never giving up hope nor abandoning me. Finally, my last missing memories found their place, each person their name! Oh, how I've missed this air."

The entire runway was empty, just like the day when I was found abandoned in the middle of it. There was no spectacular welcome here, which suggested something special might await him in the valley. The bright tunnel was lit up, but instead of music, there was a silence that allowed our voices and steps to echo to the valley as we made our way through.

When we left the tunnel, you could hear Rudolf scream, "Now," and thousands of lanterns started to float into the snowy orange sky—some of them into the bright day, others into the snow blizzard.

Each part of the Winter Lands participated, making the view spectacular and unforgettable. There was just the crackling sound of burning lanterns in the air. Each lantern had been hand made over the years, representing the hope and wishes all the citizens of the Winter Lands had nursed through the years. Wistful tears, lost smiles, prayers, all were let go after twenty years of not giving up on Santa Claus. For that is who he truly was.

"Santa is back!"

"Sean, welcome back."

"Santa!"

Somewhere in the middle of the commotion, Brian came to me.

"Victoria, I owe you an explanation." He didn't sound confident in my reaction, but I surprised even myself with my response.

"Brian. I owe you one too. But not now. There is time for everything. Now it's about Sean."

He smiled, then nodded in agreement. It was hard enough to talk anyway with all the noise.

"Victoriaaaaaaa!" Rudolf screamed so loudly his voice took over everyone else's as he sprinted toward me not caring who he knocked out of his way. The entire Chipmunk Squad fell down.

"Oh, take it easy. Glad to see you again, Ruddie."

Rudolf didn't allow me to say another word.

He whispered in my ear. "I knew it. No, I was absolutely completely sure this job was made for you and no one else. I am so happy I could hug . . . a bunny!" He did indeed go to the closest bunny, but then stopped. "Let's just pretend I did."

Rudolf jumped around until he saw Grandpa A approaching. "A family reunion after twenty years! I think I might cry like a baby," Rudolf whispered quietly to Brian and me.

The reunion of the century happened in front of the entire Winter Lands. We stood silently, watching two men silently shake hands. Only the closest of us saw Grandpa A wiping his tears away.

"Brothers will never forget about each other." A little beaver next to my legs was sobbing. "What a scene!"

"Those two are *brothers*?" No one had bothered to tell me. I realized they probably hadn't told me so I wouldn't be under more pressure, but I guess I hadn't asked either.

Cadelia was much more open in showing love to Sean.

"Oh, Sean! After twenty years! Now we all look alike. You're not the young guy anymore," She was joking because Santa Claus traditionally aged at a slower pace. Today her heart was clearly bursting with delight.

Rudolf, who was standing next to me, started to explain the story that was older than either of us. "You see, Sean and A worked together, side by side for many years. As you witnessed, there is a lot of work behind everything that goes on in the Winter Lands, so having two brothers synchronized and in charge was the best thing that ever happened to us. But two weeks before that unforgettable Christmas—twenty years ago when Sean got lost, it was the first time brothers didn't go on the trip together. Cadelia is so happy to see Sean is because she always felt guilty over what happened, since she was the reason A stayed behind. But that isn't fair to her; she only felt that way because she got sick, almost ending up in the hospital, which was what made Grandpa A stay here and take care of her. There was a clause the brothers had signed saying they would never part, so in order not to leave his wife, Grandpa A had to renounce his contract, and Sean was on his own to use the Winter Lands portals, which was unprecedented.

."Maybe it's not fair to think of it like this, but sometimes I wonder if that was what pushed Sean over the edge and made him completely lose his memory. Probably he didn't feel safe enough to use the magic alone, but he failed to communicate it to the rest of us."

By the looks on our faces, I think Grandpa A knew precisely what we were talking about with Rudolf. I didn't wait for him to come to me; I ran like a child into his arms.

"Grandpa A, I did it! Thank you for believing in me!" Emotions were pouring out of me, and I couldn't stop them; actually, I didn't want to stop them. I was overjoyed.

Later that night, I fell asleep feeling happy.

In the morning, Cadelia's voice erupted throughout the house, calling us to breakfast. Sean was staying with us in the same house, but he had left early and was already visiting the Christmas Industry Zone, trying to keep up with the progress that had taken place in his absence.

Instead of walking, I slid down the stairs, almost flying into the Christmas tree, which was now decorated with a new set of ornaments representing the winter season. Apparently Cadelia was well-known for changing her styles every few months.

"Blueberry pancakes with maple syrup are already on the table."

It seemed I might have overslept longer than I thought, Brian was already eating his breakfast.

"Good morning." Greeting Brian made my face color yet again as I looked more at the floor than at him. "You could've woken me up earlier." He had a room right next to mine.

Brian didn't lower his gaze. On the contrary, those two marvelous eyes were leading me to act childishly. I was scared of my own feelings, and knew he could probably sense it.

"I wasn't quite sure if you wanted me to." His honesty and directness were among his best qualities—but that was also why he had made my soul feel naked, exposed only to him, from the day we had met. "Victoria, I know I hid things from you, messed up your tickets, kissed you in disguise. But everything I did was for the greater good. Remember? The little adventure you had while trying to get to Chairman Ryan? That was filled with little lies for the greater good." He tried to continue, even though he knew Cadelia could hear us from the kitchen, but I stopped him because I was ready to forgive him if he just answered one question.

"Brian, I understand and I'm not angry. You don't need to apologize for the same thing I did to you." Blood rushed into my cheeks. " I have only one question: would you have shown up at one point in my life?"

Cadelia walked in with scrambled eggs, but that didn't stop Brian from replying.

"Yes." He answered without any hesitation. "Why are you asking me such a question when you can feel the answer yourself? And although you're still disappointed in how I handled our breakup, I know for a fact you're aware of the feelings I had for you since our first handshake almost ten years ago. Don't pretend otherwise."

That was it. He left me feeling speechless, embarrassed, and loved all in one. There was nothing much to add because it felt so real, and there was no space left for denial.

Cadelia interrupted. "You kids. Overcomplicating things that could've been so simple from the start with just an honest conversation." She smiled, having given her motherly advice. Now it was my turn to reply to Brian through my answer to Cadelia.

"I don't think we complicated it too much, just enough to discover what and who we really want in our lives. And, at last, we did."

Nothing could break the connection between Brian and me—not the smell of the pancakes, children's laughter, or Cadelia's proximity.

"Cadelia, do you mind if I join Rudolf and Grandpa A in visiting the facilities? There's someone I want Brian to meet at Gift Your All Workshop."

I wanted to see Addie, Little Warrior, just to see the brilliant light shining around her again. And Nora's braveness, with the rest of the marvelous kids.

Cadelia' expression suddenly changed.

"Of course you may, no need to ask. Only, I was never good in delivering sad news, but I guess it has to be me . . .. You want to see Addie again? That little warrior is not among us anymore but watching over us instead. I'm so sorry. It happened shortly after you went back to New York, the poor little one."

My brain refused to process the information. It was as though I couldn't understand the words Cadelia was saying because they seemed like a foreign language.

I only truly started to understand the words when Brian took me gently by the shoulders, bringing me back to reality, while Cadelia continued to speak: "Little Warrior has left us completely, Victoria. Now she's laughing at our adventures from above as if they are her own, each step of the way."

The truth was Addie had felt it all along, inside her, but she had stayed strong for her parents and each person whose heart she touched during her short but sweet life; she knew what we adults were scared to say out loud.

Although I wasn't entitled to have a reaction so severe for a girl I had known only for a few moments, my body collapsed into a chair, taken not by sadness, but a void in my heart. I asked myself how life could take such a beautiful soul, full of joy, from her parents and friends and from us—the world.

I needed some time to process the sad news. Eventually I managed to make myself smile in her honor because that was the only way I could pay my respects. That was continuing what she had wanted while we were talking and playing in Where Pines Stand Tall.

"Victoria, I don't intend to sound heartless, you know I would never, but she would want you to be with Sean today, for the toymaker is on his way. You are the one who found Santa Claus, and we all believe he will feel relaxed with you at his side. That's a normal thing in a situation like this."

Cadelia was right. If those kids could fight off the bad no matter what the outcome was, I could also overcome things for the greater good.

As I rushed to get ready, I was hit with new ideas I wanted to present to both brothers. As usual, my unsteady thoughts were going at a hundred miles per hour.

"How could that slip my mind? I'm not prepared," I muttered. As I continued stressing, Brian tried to calm me down.

"Go get dressed, and don't worry, I will go with you both!"

I don't know how anyone could ever refuse his smile.

Sean's cheerful voice sang through the hallway: "Victoria, are you ready?"

We ran down as fast as we could. "Born ready."

"New information has been shared with us in the last minute. The toymaker is bringing his silent partner to help him make a final decision. Unfortunately, until today, we have never had the chance to meet him in person, as maybe he could've helped our situation without involving my friend's company." He couldn't hide his terror of meeting with this person who didn't believe in anything magical or extraordinary.

"Why does he need a silent partner?"

Sean didn't understand that part either. "Brian is our consultant for that kind of business, but apparently the man is remarkably good at his job. He brought in investors and saved their company a couple of times over the past ten years. I would know more if I had been present. But what can I do? We have to work with what we know. For now." He winked at me.

There was nothing we could do but fight for the survival of the toy industry in the Winter Lands with heads held high.

"We have to hurry. Come on. They are already waiting for us in the Crystal Room in the Andes."

"I don't wanna slow us down, but we are currently under the

Dolomites range. How can we travel so fast to South America? Two times I came here, it was with a plane and somehow I doubt that's the fastest way of traveling Winter Lands can offer."

A lot of things were left unexplained since my last visit here.

Brian jumped in to explain. "You see those transparent, seemingly perpetual 'tubes'? Those are called RushUp Tubes, not so long ago I learned they use them to change destinations between the continents in the shortest time possible. One of the Winter Lands technological breakthroughs. There are different speeds of transportation, where the fastest one is the most uncomfortable due to the high velocity, uncomfortable vibrations, and high-pitched sound. All things considered, somehow, animals take it much better than us."

"Amazing! Suspended in a thin air, we are going to *rush* at high velocity through the tubes? Wow. Not my favorite ride for sure."

Meanwhile, Sean kept talking into the walkie-talkie, nervously walking up and down.

Apparently, Grandpa A had sent news that the toymaker didn't seem impressed with anything, and was visibly irritated that he had had to come all the way to the mountains to negotiate. Grandpa A didn't like the toymaker at all.

"He's the sort of man who can't see far in front of his nose." He said.

Sean seemed perplexed. "Victoria, I am afraid to see the eyes of my old friend, reflected in his son's look, while he tells me why he doesn't want to continue with the life-long collaboration his father and I established."

I took Sean's hand in mine. "We got this. After everything we've been through, don't you think?" Sean clearly wanted to believe me, but that look of apprehension still didn't leave his face.

# Lightning Strike of Destiny

Grandpa A's reports were a little discouraging to Sean. He muttered that he had never heard of a man unimpressed by the beauties of the Winter Lands.

Sean had forgotten that the toymaker and the partner were actually thinking they were in the Andes. Judging by Sean's expression, disappointment clouded his mind. He wondered out loud what had happened to the toymaker that made him stop believing in beautiful things:

"I guess living in the city for twenty years showed me exactly how life there sometimes sends a person into a negative state of mind, confused by situations, cheered up only by material, touchable goods."

Once we got there, Rudolf couldn't go inside. He wasn't allowed to approach the Aurora Hall, partly because of an old accident that had left him traumatized as a cub—unfortunately, people from the outside couldn't see him as we did. To them, he was a just an animal whose roars they couldn't understand, so one of them had thrown a crystal vase at the bear cub, scarring him for life, just because they were unable to accept someone different than them. That was the last time Winter Lands ever tried to persuade outsiders with a talking animal. So, Rudolf went up with the fastest RushUp Tube, not waiting for us, just to peek through the window of the great hall to see what the toymaker was doing.

He was talking with us through a walkie-talkie.

"Apparently, he asked for water, Victoria." Sean was outraged when the news came in. "Not juice, hot chocolate, coffee, or tea? No. Simple, plain water, and he even seems disgusted with that too. Maybe it's because it doesn't have a brand on it. Fresh things don't suit him, clearly."

It was scary to go up in the RushUp Tube because, apart from the mountains, everything else was made from transparent materials, so it didn't interfere with nature's beauty. It almost felt like we were suspended in the air on nothing more than cozy pillows with safety belts.

The Crystal Slides were a chain of mountains made of the Himalayas, Dolomites, Alps, Rocky Mountains, and Andes. All the wonders nature gave us, connected in one spot, under the beautiful Aurora Borealis, creating a world inside a world. Standing at the base of those mountains, I felt so small.

Towering and sharp mountain peaks were penetrating a dense fog and clouds in an indescribably eerie, yet magnificent way. Even if there were no lights in Aurora Hall, the mountain would still have been shining brightly with its diamond-white snow. Against that scenery, it seemed like there were no problems, just solutions, and nothing felt impossible. I wished I could feel like that every day.

Sean noticed the childish marvel in my eyes.

"If you think this is something, wait until we get to the top." A tiny smile broke through his worried expression.

Once we made it, I saw that Sean was completely right. We came to one spot from which we could clearly see that all the mountains were linked with the Crystal Hallways, passageways for RushUp Tubes, which looked like thin shiny threads from afar, reflecting the sky's colors.

Of course, I was amazed by the technology that must have lain behind such creations. I had learned from Rudolf to leave some things to the charm of the moment rather than questioning them.

Each lightning bolt we saw on these mountains meant something new was emerging from the attractiveness of the lightning and snow. In this case, the RushUp Tubes were made from the crystals coming from those mountains.

Our meeting was to take place on the fifth chain, the Andes. It took us only fifteen minutes to pass the other four chains. I didn't even want to know the velocity of our RushUp Tube. We could feel the slightly uncomfortable vibrations.

"Sean, I am speechless." I was delighted by the crystal vaults and the speed of our transition from mountain to mountain, with the help of the crystal tube inside which we sat on fluffy pillows on a flat surface, much like the conveyor belt you find at airports.

Brian was sitting still and smiling.

"This was your goal, Vicky. You can finally enjoy the heights without the fear. I think the RushUp Tubes are perfect for you."

And he was right.

Sean's hands were uncontrollably shaking. Was he was afraid he had been out of the picture too long to handle this important meeting the right way?

I felt an urge to step in. "Santa . . ." Calling him that sounded so sweet. "You did this for many years. You got this."

The Crystal Hallway that took us to Aurora Hall was mesmerizing, with a thousand little details and various snowflake patterns all over the walls and floor. A big crystal room in the middle of the mountain reflected everything from the outside onto the interior's design.

Ice Harris was also here, to help us measure the levels of belief and happiness present in the room. Judging by his heart's faded color, things didn't seem to be going well. At the end of the hall, there were three people sitting and waiting for us at a long oak table under an enormous chandelier made of crystal raindrops that never stopped rotating.

"I guess it is time." Sean clasped my hand and took a deep breath. It was like being on that bench in Central Park all over again, as both of us were anxious and uncertain but hopeful.

As we approached the silent group, I was still petrified. My head felt like it was starting to spin around, making me hold onto Sean. Grandpa A was already seated with the toymaker and his silent partner.

"Victoria." One of the men at the table stood up, surprised.

"Dad?" I barely managed to speak.

Sean was frantically looking back and forward from the man to me. "Victoria?"

My stomach was in a massive knot, twitching nervously, because I knew this was the worst thing that could happen. Not only did I feel miserable for having lied to Dad so many times in a short period—no lie was justified, especially not so many in a row—but also I knew this could ruin everything Santa was hoping for.

Then time stopped, and I actually fainted at some point. Brian and Sean were helping me to fend off Dad's attempts to take me back home with him. I don't recall what happened next, but afterward I was told that the toymaker had announced, as expected, the deal was off with his business and material supplies, that my father had left without saying another word to me—not that I could've listened in my condition—and above all, they had both said they weren't crazy enough to work with a place that couldn't be explained anywhere in the papers or to their other investors. Rudolf told me that my father had screamed at me while I stood there, pale, not really understanding what was going on around me. Then I began to scream words at him without making sense.

After the meeting, Sean and Brian took me outside to be brought back around by the freezing air. They comforted me in my state of shock, and kept repeating it wasn't my fault.

This turn of events surprised me so much that I was wasn't aware of anything around me for quite some time. My joy had turned to shock.

Now, Rudolf joined them in comforting me while Grandpa A ran after my father before he went home to try to explain things.

But Brian's voice was the first to get to me.

"And if you could speak? What would you say? How would he react? It was on us, our mistake for not checking on who the silent partner was. The Winter Lands never usually take those things for granted. But with Santa coming back and all the festivities . . . Normally, some things were overlooked."

I understood what he was saying, but that didn't stop me from feeling torn. I couldn't help but cry.

"Oh, Vicky, don't cry. You're breaking my heart." Rudolf hugged me. "Everything will be just fine."

Sean came up with an inspired but risky idea: "You will get home before your father does, and I do mean a long time before. That way, your mom and sister will be witnesses of your presence at home. Don't forget Vicky, your dad actually flew to South America and for him, this was a strange but real meeting in Peru. He still needs to go to the hotel, book an earlier flight, drive to the airport . . . Your father won't be able to understand how that could happen, nor the fact that the day he saw you here was the same day when you returned home within an hour! Then you will have the opportunity to explain him the situation—without actually revealing the truth of the Winter Lands."

I asked how I could do that if there was a restriction on what was shareable and what was not.

"Easy, you just have to convince him to believe in something he can't see. *You found me.* What is this to you, Victoria?"

They both tried hard, but at this point, nothing was making much sense.

Then Brian tried to find the sense out of everything.

"Victoria, I don't want to push it, but maybe this situation between you and your dad was meant to happen . . ."

"Now *you* aren't making sense."

"Listen," Brian started carefully, "it was inevitable that Sean would lose this toymaker—we basically lost the contract as soon as the toymaker announced the business would be restructured. He is the main investor so he had the final say, he just came here out of respect toward his father and Sean. And the story would have ended there. No one could do anything about it. Are you following me? It would've finished in the Crystal Room, and we would have had to start back from ground zero right before Christmas. I don't know if you paid attention, but we don't have more time. Christmas is in twelve days."

He was constantly checking if I was with him, and I nodded my head.

"Okay. Now, it happens their silent partner, who is responsible for the company's success, was none other than your dad, someone we know. Someone *you* know really well. So, if you can somehow, in that crazy weird way of yours, convince him to help us find a new big toymaking company, and to convince other toymakers we work with to continue our collaboration; maybe everything isn't lost for the Winter Lands."

I knew he might be right.

"And the bright side of it? You don't have to break into your own house to talk with the man." His joke relieved my stress and helped to tame my emotional hurricane, so I offered him a weak smile.

I had the power in me to turn this into something good.

Brian had always entered my life exactly when I needed him the most. He was my Mary Poppins and he was finally here to stay.

"Now," he said. "Let me take you to my favorite place on Earth, before night falls!"

"But it's already dark."

Brian smiled mysteriously. "Not where I'm taking you."

So, shortly after that, we took a sleigh ride to Brian's special place, and that alone was an adventure, one that I don't have time to tell you about here; I'll never be too old for reindeer and sleighs, and there are too many wonders in the Winter Lands to be described.

From complete darkness, we gradually entered the dusk. It was as though someone had just painted more brightness into the day.

And then I saw it, and I realized my next bucket list item could be checked off.

"This is Rakotzbrücke? The bridge in Germany?"

In front of us, with nothing but a lake standing in between, was the most precise manmade bridge. Together with its reflection in the water, the bridge created a perfect circle. People called it "Devil's Bridge",but I never considered it such. All I saw was the beautiful perfection a human mind created—free of any limitations, fulled with the conviction in their own ideas.

With snow covering the trees around it, Rakotzbrücke seemed wonderful. People's dreams of leaving a mark behind them were much stronger in the past; you could witness that in its architecture. Each stone, small or big, the spiral tubes on the sides, and even the clean reflections were carefully planned and executed—I do believe people in the past rarely said "no" or heard "you can't" for an answer.

The scene almost looked like a picture.

Brian smiled at me for no apparent reason.

"There is a reason why we're here alone, isn't there?" I wasn't surprised. Actually, in a weird way, I felt relaxed now.

"Did you doubt it?"

"Since Rudolf, Grandpa A, and Sean have their hands full preparing everything for each Christmas headquarters, and everything has to be ready starting December twenty-first, they gave me the honor of showing you something they use only, and I do underline *only*, in emergencies, which of course this situation is. A little bird told me you have been asking about the magic a lot. Okay, this bridge looks pretty, but it is also a loop in space. It was discovered a long time ago. The bridge was built almost one hundred and sixty years ago. But its magical powers were discovered about a hundred years ago when a tourist walked over the bridge and found himself in Cairo, Egypt. Of course, no one believed him, and the world proclaimed him crazy but years later that story came to Winter Lands. It turned out to be true. This space loop is one of a kind, marked by this amazing piece of architecture that takes you wherever you want to go just by crossing it. But no one knows what was first: the loop or the architecture."

After everything that had happened to me lately, this didn't seem so strange.

"Do I have to jump off it?"

"What do you think this is, a fairy tale? Of course not. I already told you to cross it. From the Winter Lands, you have to cross the bridge with the picture of the place you want to go held sharp in your mind. It has to be in nature only. The water reflection in the exact middle loops over you, so by the end of the walk across, you're in the destination you wished for. Here, they don't use it often, rarely actually," he added quietly, knowing I wouldn't miss it, "because of how tricky it can sometimes be."

Brian left it unsaid, but I instinctively grasped what the danger was.

"There is a chance my memories could stay behind me, isn't there? That's why I see those little candle-shaped lights on the pine branches. One for each person who left this way without finding their way back home."

"That's right. You have to seriously feel this moment as truth, Vicky. It is the only way not to lose this land and your sanity. I wish I could help you more, but—"

I didn't take a lot of convincing. "I want to do it. If it is the only way to get home quickly enough, I have to do it. Now." I also knew that I either had to do this while I still could, or stay here petrified with fear.

"It is. Let's get you on your way."

"Wherever I want to? For example, Central Park, the closest thing to my house?"

"Why not?"

Suddenly, I stopped before crossing the bridge. My mind had flooded with last-minute doubt.

"Can I have the picture of the park on your phone while walking? It would help me a lot. I left my phone with Joanna!" My cheeks were embarrassed red; but Brian just giggled and handed it over.

"Anything that helps."

❄

On the bridge, I took one last look at Brian. There was no kiss good-bye, nothing, because we both knew I'd be back sooner than Rudolf could correctly pronounce the word *magnificent*, even though his unsuccessful attempts were funny.

I nervously held the phone between my fingers—it seemed as if my hands were sweating even though it was quite cold.

The view from the top of the bridge was indescribably unique. The cold breeze suddenly disappeared, and the snow stopped; white fluffy clouds opened up a bright spot in the skies, giving light to the moment.

I could hear Brian's voice far away, echoing as though he was inside a tunnel, telling me to keep walking, which I did, spurred on by his faded words. Somewhere on my way down the hill, I started to feel a warm, fuzzy, altogether strange feeling overwhelming my body, tingling my senses until it made me chuckle out of joy. And then, in the end, I found myself walking off the small bridge in Central Park.

Home.

The picture on Brian's cell phone exactly matched the spot I was standing. At this moment I felt happy and relieved that he had a cool background picture of my favorite park on hand. When I thought of everything that could have gone wrong, I was seized by the immensity of what could have gone wrong.

Now, having experienced even more impossible things, confronting my father seemed an easy task to do, so my heart filled with hope.

I ran into the building faster than Walter could say hi to me.

Joanna opened the door. "Already here? But it hasn't even been two full days yet. Never mind, I had so much fun playing with your phone." She continued to jump happily around me, even helping me take my coat off, which usually didn't happen unless she had some secret agenda. "When are you going to tell me where you were? What happened? You seem worried. Is it boy-related? Please tell me." She caught her breath for a moment, only to continue with more questions.

Meanwhile, I was still trying to take off my boots.

"Please, Victoria." Her voice calmed a notch. "I was really good, did everything you asked me. Overall, I did my best. By the way, Mom and Dad suspect nothing."

Maybe it was her sweet demeanor I wasn't used to, perhaps it was the exhaustion of running around, or maybe I was just tired of lying, but somehow the complete truth just slipped out. "You are, unfortunately, wrong. Dad saw me in the middle of the Andes. Yes, in South America, a really long way from home."

For the first time, Joanna was at a loss for words.

My first instinct was to tell her it was only a joke, but I just couldn't lie anymore. She didn't deserve it in the first place, and she was my family, so I started from the beginning without waiting for her to rain any more questions down on me.

She listened carefully, absorbing every detail. It took a while, and when I finished what, even to me, sounded like an invented story, and *I* had lived it, she spoke, "Do you have pictures?"

"Well, I gave you my phone, didn't I? I simply refuse to believe you didn't snoop through my albums out of curiosity. Never mind, listen."

Then I told her about the Winter Lands: their rules, how the pictures of their landscape in my phone were real. Joanna didn't pay any special attention to them since she thought I downloaded a bunch of winter pictures just to change my cellphone background.

Joanna listened until the very end. "You have to take me there some day. Promise! I might even start believing in Santa Claus again. It's never too late, and you're my proof!"

I was amazed by her reaction, though I couldn't figure out if she really believed me or only was playing along because she had nothing to add.

When my mom heard us talking, she came into the room to see what was going on. She was acting normally, greeting me enthusiastically with a smile and asking about how my studying had gone, and I didn't lie.

"Everything is great, Mom."

"Please help me with the cleaning. Your dad is coming tomorrow at ten in the morning and he is having a meeting here, but I won't be able to help with anything."

"Mom, don't worry. I'll help him." It surprised her I offered to be involved in his business, but she let it be.

The whole night I was turning around in my bed, waking up every hour to check on the time. And as the arrival of my dad grew closer, my nerves naturally got the better of me. I knew he didn't have a work meeting at home. He never mixed those two things.

He probably needed that time to absorb what had happened, and perhaps to create scenarios in his head so he could explain to my mother that he had seen their daughter in the remote mountains of South America.

In bed, lying down with my eyes closed, I thought about everything that had happened in my life and tried to figure out what I could have done better or different. But I always saw myself doing the same things, over and over, taking the exact same approach.

# Do You Believe in Good?

I was home alone, waiting for this moment, knowing Dad was about to witness a confusing surprise. Mom had told me that he had taken the first flight he could get to New York, so there was physically no way I could have beaten him here in the real world.

Joanna had gone to school, and Mom to meet her publisher to coordinate a new book signing.

A key turned in the lock. The sound was crisp and clear throughout the entire house.

"Victoria?" He virtually hissed my name through his teeth, and looked as though he was seeing a ghost. "No! I saw you there. You were there in Peru! H—how? No. Impossible. You were there."

He couldn't say two normal sentences in a row. I had already prepared water with sugar to calm his nerves so I handed him a glass.

"You were there. I saw you!" He couldn't stop repeating himself.

No more lies.

"Yes, I was. But I came home yesterday afternoon. If you don't believe me, and you have every right not to, then ask Mom and Joanna. I spent the whole day with them, and at least you know *they* wouldn't lie to you." My harsh tone seemed to increase his level of anxiety.

His strong voice cracked. "Yesterday? But that's not possible. No. NO!"

Everyone knew my father as a calm person who never reacted to anything, but now he lost control for the second time in just a few days.

"Why is it impossible? Because it would imply you'd have to believe in the impossible, right? Yet here I am, from yesterday afternoon."

"The only explanation is that I'm going crazy."

"Then we are both crazy. Let me explain."

Well, I couldn't tell him the entire truth. Joanna was my wild card. I had promised Sean I would make my father believe by showing him how many people still believed in the goodness of a heart. So I could tell Dad about my connection to Sean within certain limitations; how I had helped him regain his memories and find his hometown, how I had flown on a private jet, how I had started a relationship with Brian, who also worked with Sean and me on our special projects in a fantastic town no one knew about . . . but there was nothing about the loop bridge or the talking bear and I didn't mention the name of the Winter Lands. Those things were left unsaid because the truth wasn't easy to embrace, but at least what I did tell him made his imagination tingle with possibilities.

I mentioned right away I was there in the hope of saving the partnership that would help us do so much more to help kids around the world.

Like Joanna, he didn't say a word after I told him this story.

I didn't have to wait long for the traditional parent part to kick in though.

"Going away on a private jet, working pro bono for the same company I used to work with, and doing it secretly behind our back. Even your one-week boyfriend knew, and I didn't. What if anything happened to you?"

"Nothing happened to me. I know you are confused, but . . . "

"Stop with the 'I know, but.' It's no use apologizing for things you did deliberately; just stop and take responsibility for it."

Although he was partly right and we both knew it, I was angry at him too because I knew life wasn't black and white; it had all varieties of colors.

"Dad, I *am* sorry for not telling you stuff when I was supposed to, but that is only because you and Mom give me such strict rules, even though I am twenty-six years old. And if I had told you about my plans, or the job I took, then you'd probably have locked me in the room and tried to make me come to my senses. Am I right, Dad?"

"Don't start."

"No. Dad, you want honesty? Let's be honest then. I admitted for the hundredth time you were right. Now it's your turn, am I right?" Giving up on this wasn't an option.

However, he refused to listen to my words, ignoring me completely, and kept trying to play the strong dad role. He talked about all I had done lately and the drastic change I'd been through over the last couple of months. He even implied that Brian was probably to blame for my involvement in the business. In the middle of his nonsensical monologue, I stopped listening to what he had to say because I knew that every word was being said out of anger. Those words could've hurt my feelings if I had kept listening.

After a while, rather than taking it anymore, I abruptly interrupted his speech.

I had that gut feeling in my stomach again: it was twisted up, but in good knots.

"Dad, when you came to the meeting the other day, did you even stop and try to really look at the crystal walls of the room, the sculptures, or even the floor you were standing on?" I sounded so determined, I managed to regain his attention for a moment.

"Excuse me?" He was playing for time, but I knew he had heard what I had asked.

"Did you stand in Aurora Hall asking yourself if the light inside was a real reflection and why it got that name? Like, did you allow yourself to look beyond the bounds of ordinary reason? Did you wonder why your meeting about toys and materials was being held in the middle of nowhere?"

My dad looked at me, momentarily amazed, and perhaps slightly embarrassed.

That's when I was sure my dad had seen something extraordinary about the meeting.

"There had to be at least a glimpse of something unusual you just couldn't rationally explain, but after a while of dwelling on it, you just accepted in your mind the form in which it presented itself. Am I right?"

I finally saw a shadow of memory crossing his expression. We both looked at each other, knowing the truth.

His numb silence was clear confirmation.

And then a great idea suddenly hit me. Yesterday while running home, my eye had caught sight of a flyer about today's Central Park gathering for homeless children. It was handwritten, probably from some small organization or shelter not funded well enough to allow for printed flyers, but that didn't make it any less important. On the contrary, people had to show unconditional love and affection to work for such an organization.

"Wait here for a second."

I ran to the drawer in my room to take out every greeting card I had at my disposal with customized wishes as well as money. I had kept these so I could prepare them for random passersby for Christmas Eve, so I could at least make people's holidays happier with a small gesture. Even though it was still early in December, I was going to make a bet with my dad about how many people were ready to donate their time or their gifts for good deeds nowadays, without knowing what it was for.

Faith without evidence.

I piled the money on the table in front of my dad.

"Are you trying to bribe me now?" Dad joking was a good sign I had gotten through to him at least a bit.

I started carefully.

"Dad, I am . . . No, *we* are going to do something exceptional now . . . we are going out together and put our fate in other people's hands. If I manage to show you people are still capable of trust and goodwill without being given any information about what we are doing and who we are doing it for, are you ready to promise not only to forgive me, but also to find a new company for Sean Christmas as well as the investors this year? And you don't have a lot of time on your hands. Christmas is around the corner."

He looked at me suspiciously. "That is very bold of you. Why would I ever say yes to that kind of a deal?"

"Dad. There are things I have promised not to say, and promises are not to be broken. You taught me that, remember? All I need in this game of ours is your time. Afterward, you will understand why your daughter, who always seemed so calm, does the strangest things in the hardest way imaginable. That behavior has been there in me from a young age. It is who I am. I could feel other people's pain, joy, anxiety, their most secret emotions. You saw me in the Andes the other day, and now I am here. Crazy stuff happened, and then there was Rakotzbrücke." I got lost slightly while recalling the memories. "But that is another story . . . Like Chairman Ryan, Sean Christmas chose me out of all the people in this world to collaborate with him on everything. It is nothing I'll be able to explain without complicating it and confusing you, trust me. If I can make at least 1111 people come to an event in the park with simple words of love and mystery, and together with those envelopes, will you do what I asked of you?"

I didn't overthink the things I've said, but he was listening to my proposal carefully.

"Why that specific number?"

"'1111' is known as *angel number,* and it reminds me of a good friend whose house is full of angle motifs."

There was that awkward undesirable silence again. Like every business person out there, my dad had to consider every factor before coming to a conclusion.

"Help me understand. You're going to fill these envelopes with money and cards, obviously, and hand them over to strangers in the street expecting more than a hundred of them to show up to donate to an unknown recipient in the heart of Central Park in the middle of a workday? Okay."

He nodded in agreement but couldn't stop from offering a sarcastic follow up:

"I just bet they'll all show up."

His comment didn't bother me. I was filled with adrenalin from the excitement that we were finally doing a beautiful thing together. That alone convinced me people would show up.

After almost forty-five minutes of putting cards and money together with my dad, we were ready to test my claims. There were all kinds of bills, randomly put inside the cute cards, with and an address and time where to take them.

*Today.*
*Sheep Meadow, Central Park.*
*At 3:00 pm.*
*Spread the word!*

There was a side note also telling people it's ok if they use the money for themselves.

In the lobby, Walter was putting his coat on, ready to go home to his new place.

"Vicky, can I give you another hug? I can never thank you enough for what you did for our family."

He didn't really need to ask if he could hug me, but maybe he didn't want to offend my dad by doing it. I ran to his arms, and he started telling my dad about his new home as we hugged.

"Walter, would you join Dad and me on a little quest? Trust me when I say it will pay off in the most wonderful way."

I didn't share any more information, but Walter cheerfully agreed to go with us. "When that girl has something on her mind, she'll do whatever it takes to make it happen," he said to my dad.

Soon afterward I stopped the first people in front of the Plaza. They were an elderly couple holding hands while rolling suitcases with the other. They were entering the hotel to check in for their first vacation to New York from Germany, after forty years of marriage. They told me this straightforwardly, they had just been waiting to talk to someone here in America. As ever, it was true that happy people bonded faster than all the rest.

"In the spirit of the upcoming holiday, can I gift you this card with something small inside?" They weren't shy, so the envelope was opened right before us.

"Forty dollars? That is so kind, what a welcome to this country." The woman came straight to me for a hug.

"You can use it as you wish. Or, if you want to experience real love powered by pure gratitude and endless childish joy, you can come with those cards to Central Park meadow, any time after four o'clock in the afternoon, and use it to gift Christmas to someone else. No one will judge you, and no one will know what happened here. We plan to distribute as many of these as we can, and I trust your choice entirely." After I said that, the German couple didn't understand some of the words, so my dad jumped in to explain in German. He was great, but even so he left them utterly confused.

"What will happen in Central Park?"

I shrugged my shoulders. "Your good will and trust in something you don't have control over. The only thing I can tell you is that by coming there, you will gift not only this card with the money but also your precious time for a genuine moment of love. We have to go now. If I don't see you again, happy holidays and may your days be blessed with happiness."

The cute German couple kept looking from me to my dad and Walter, but they didn't say anything, just gave a polite nod with their heads and then proceeded to the check-in desk. The words I said had to be repeated from the heart to each person we decided to stop, and the three of us soon got the hang of it. Walter and Dad started to relax into the role, even though they didn't know why they were doing it or who it was for. Nevertheless, they had decided to trust me, so they stopped each person, no matter their age, gender, race, or clothes. And the best part came in between when we heard people talking about what we were doing, without knowing us. New York was a big city, crowded with tourists as well as locals, but that didn't stop people from sharing what they had seen or heard here with their friends, families, or anyone they were passing. We still weren't sure if there would be more than thousand people, but we were confident of one thing: good news travels fast.

Two mothers on the sidewalk of 59th Street were talking about a mysterious movement that guaranteed everyone pure happiness.

"I have to be honest with you, Jessica, today was supposed to be my first day of shopping, which I love beyond anything else. But now I'm intrigued by this secret meeting, and I'm taking my kids to the park instead." The story did seem to be spreading quickly, but people were adding stuff or words to it we never mentioned, making it bigger and better, well, sometimes worse, and hopefully as crowded as I expected.

"When is that?"

"Around 3:00 p.m., I think."

The tall lady shook her head, clearly unconvinced. "Oh God . . . Talking about joy and tears . . . that is totally not my thing."

The three of us laughed as we heard her. Once stories started to spread, they did change from person to person.

"If I decide to go, with some money . . . I would want to feel safe. Let me Google it first to see if I can find it under events. Maybe it's a promotion for somebody's concert. Cheap stuff, you know."

We heard a lot of different things during the day; some of them positive, some stupid, but nothing compared to my mom's call at noon.

"Yes?"

"What on earth is going on with you and your dad? Walter too. Did you go nuts? The three of you are all over Instagram, Facebook, and even that strange Snap-something stuff . . . Where are you inviting people to, and why wasn't I invited?"

I couldn't handle her anger and faked jealous feelings right now, and I wasn't ready to tell her what I had told Dad, so I handed the phone to him.

At least there were no more lies on my part that way.

"Thanks a lot," he added sarcastically while my mom screamed my name on the other end.

If my mom knew, then Joanna probably knew too. I mean, in school, social media was everything these days.

Not only were people thinking about regifting their gift, calling the movement "Gift Christmas," which I was proud of, but they were also ready to come somewhere on a pure belief they will experience promised happiness.

That was Belief. That was Faith.

That was the kind of curiosity that could change the world for the better.

# The Final Chapter to
# New Beginnings

At 3:00 p.m., Dad and I went to Central Park, while Walter went home to get his wife and bring her along. As we approached the gathering for homeless children, my heart jumped a bit from joy as I saw beautiful kids playing in an improvised, worn-out Santa's village. They didn't care what it looked like as long as it was something to play in. They were trying to call the passerby to join them in their games.

Now my dad started questioning what this was all about. Naturally, he wanted to know who we did it for. "Who are those kids?"

Walter, who joined us again with his wife, had already worked out what was going on here today, thanks to his wife, so he shared it with my dad.

"Why didn't you just explain to people about those kids?" Dad asked me a logical question, but I was prepared for that.

"Because, that wasn't the deal we made: I promised to show you people still believe in the unknown, that they do trust people without any concrete proof. This wasn't about knowing the details and putting people in a position to say yes or no. It was to trust that giving something away would mean receiving better, non-material things in return. How else could I prove to you that impossible things are not that impossible and that magic can happen anytime and anywhere?"

"Good point," he said, but you could still see the worry on his face. As a businessman, he was just thinking about how many more people we could've had if I had only given the exact information to attract them here to help those children.

Dealing with the business world had naturally made him more suspicious, and it is always hard to change our habits. But there was no point in talking about it anymore.

I didn't expect people to come precisely on time. After all, the children had prepared material for three hours of fun for everyone present, meaning it would last until six o'clock in the afternoon, but I couldn't calm the rapid beating inside my chest. I was literally having to tell myself when to exhale and breathe in, as I would periodically forget.

That's when someone tapped me on the shoulders. A very tall gymnastics teacher named Emma, as her name tag stated, approached me about the Christmas card donation.

"Excuse me, Miss. I'm sorry to bother you, but I just met a family from Sweden that gave me a Christmas card with twenty dollars in it, telling me three people gave it to them to bring it here to the park's event. When we've asked who told them that, they pointed at you three."

I didn't know what to say, so my dad started to explain what we were trying to do today.

The family was waiving cheerfully from the front of the stage.

Emma's expression showed she also didn't know what to say but 'thank you'.

"Can I ask you a favor? Would you like to join the kids later on the stage? All of you? Not many people are here today, so it would make kids happy to have company."

As we watched them dance, my mind was occupied by the little children as they captured me with their magical world of imagination. It was like watching them playing in the middle of the Winter Lands.

At one point, there was an announcement to say that Santa was running late to their show, so with a little help and approval from other teachers and guardians, we sat the children down and told them random stories to keep them occupied.

Young or old, they listened carefully. At the very end of a weirdly funny story that Walter and I invented, I added something important: "In a while, if you believe hard enough, two little angels will send you a lot of good people bringing help for your temporary homes, and the world will see your show and play with you."

One hand was raised up high. Although tiny in size, it was spiking out from the crowd.

"How many people?" The girl with braids spoke so sweetly. She boldly stood up so I could see her clearly. She had the cutest little black braids on the sides of her head, but her energy levels would shame a grown man.

"More than you can count." Dad stepped in, keeping it fun, and I never felt so proud.

No one was really waiting for anything. We were just trying to enjoy ourselves, but without even noticing, the park started to fill up with people asking what was happening here and who they could give the money they had been gifted to.

By 4:30 p.m. all of Central Park Meadow was covered by the river of people who were still pouring into the valley, from parents and grandparents with their grandchildren to passersby, while the children in need innocently continued with their show, not quite understanding what was going on now. The crowd numbered more than a thousand people, and it was showing no signs of stopping.

People were spreading word from mouth to mouth.

I was somewhere in between tears and laughter, as people, who remembered us, came up to congratulate on what we three had done. It was so much more than I expected, and my dad stood by my side the whole time.

"We are so proud of you." Walter and his wife were hugging me tightly, and they were joined by my dad.

And my dad? Oh, well.

"The next few days I'll spend calling a few people. Sean will have his investors and a new company by the end of this week." He didn't elaborate, but I knew he meant what he was saying.

Through the crowd I saw my mom, Joanna, some friends, and, from a different direction, Brian approaching me, all staring around at the huge crowd that had shown up in Central Park in search of happiness.

"How did—?"

Brian smiled. "I had a precise picture in my mind of where I wanted to go, so I wasn't worried at all. And—I called your mother to ask where you were. To my surprise she told me right away and we continued talking for a while. Very nice lady."

I was happy.

It was all for Sean. For the Winter Lands. For Little Addie. For Nora. For all the sick children and children without homes and real love in their lives. For them to never lose hope.

I believed in a higher good, and it paid off in a marvelous way. And all this was happening while I had the loved ones with me.

Then a familiar deep voice came from behind me.

"You did it once again." As I made a sudden clumsy turn, my arm hit Chairman Ryan's shoulder.

"Oh, I am so sorry. You startled me."

"Well, maybe I deserved it." The chairman was the only person I knew who, when he smiled with sincerity, seemed scary.

"My students told me about this crazy girl in Central Park giving away money so people could Gift Christmas to others, promising a weird feeling of utopia at a mysterious event."

I started laughing as I thought about all the ways the story had changed so far. But at the same time, I was ecstatic.

"Imagine my surprise to see you in front of me." He nodded. "But now I'm here… and I have a special offer for you, which we are going to talk about next week in my office. *Not* my house." Now I knew he was making fun of me.

"Thank you," I whispered, leaving him to enjoy the show.

My cellphone rang.

It was a call from the Winter Lands, where everyone was yelling at the same time, to the point where Sean had problems saying anything. He told me how New York Christmas headquarters told them about the river of people coming to Central Park to help the homeless children's play, and that it all started with three people in front of Plaza Athene. Apparently, they have our faces all over the news now.

"Victoria. Thank you. Thank you all." His voice sounded more cheerful than ever.

That was all he said, but it was enough.

And though it might seem like my adventure ended here, it had actually barely even started.